THE THINGS I DO FOR LOVE

The Things I Do For Love

SYDNEY PENNINGTON

iUniverse, Inc.
Bloomington

The Things I Do For Love

iUniverse books may be ordered through booksellers or by contacting:

iUniverse
1663 Liberty Drive
Bloomington, IN 47403
www.iuniverse.com
1-800-Authors (1-800-288-4677)

ISBN: 978-1-4502-9441-6 (sc)
ISBN: 978-1-4502-9442-3 (ebk)

Printed in the United States of America

iUniverse rev. date: 02/10/2011

For Danita, because she let me borrow her muse and plot bunnies when mine refused to cooperate. I love you, Sissy.

"Love is much like a wild rose, beautiful and calm, but willing to draw blood in its defense."- Mark Overby

TABLE OF CONTENTS

PREFACE

The idea for this story first came to me when my best friend Danita and I were hiking through the woods near her house. We were searching for an old barge near the Ohio River that I had found years before with some family friends. Even for thirteen year-olds, we had hyperactive and wild imaginations. We would often pretend we were someone else in complicated situations. We would completely act out our little adventures. One day, I just decided to try writing one down, and it became a book.

Almost every time we come up with something new, one of us writes it down. Some of them I try to write into stories, and she does the others. We always help each other out with writing. I sometimes call her at three in the morning when I have writers block. She is always patient with me and gives me new ideas. When I started writing this, I had no idea it would turn out the way it did. Without Danita, it would probably still be six chapters of crap written in my notebook.

Most of my characters are based off of real people. Rena has Danita's personality and Serenity has mine. Courtney is loosely based off of her little sister. I got the idea of Shorty when I was watching Scary Movie 2, and I incorporated that into the personality of one of my other best friends. Random names of my friends and family are sprinkled throughout the story. I can't really take completely full credit for this story; I've had a lot of help and encouragement. By encouragement, I mean threatening. A lot of people threatened to hurt me if I didn't finish writing, so that was some pretty good incentive.

I would like to thank Danita Fain for all of her help on this story. I couldn't have done it without her. She also did a crap load of editing on this book. I want to thank Katie S. for going through this story multiple times and doing even more editing than Danita. She was always patient with my hectic schedule and never gave up on my story. She has been like a momma bird throughout the whole process. Thanks Katie.

I want to thank my little sister, Olivia, for annoying me every chance she got and not ever having faith in me. It made me want to prove her wrong. I also want to thank my mom because she put everything she had into helping me.

CHAPTER ONE

I Won't Do It

"Serenity!" my father yelled, "come down stairs and bring Rena, I need to talk to the two of you."

Oh great. When my father needed to talk to us, it was usually something about school or when he wanted to give us new chores.

I closed my book and got off of my bed, turning off my music as I left the room. I walked across the hall to Rena's room. When I knocked on her door, I heard a loud bang come from inside. That probably meant that she was doing something she shouldn't be. It wouldn't have been the first time.

"Who is it?" Rena called as she let out a cough.

"It's Serenity. Open up!"

She opened and squeezed out the door, leaving behind a cloud of smoke; she was smoking pot again. That was so gross, and totally aggravating. I knew there was a reason, but she never told me. It was probably one of the only secrets between us. We told each other everything; we weren't just sisters, we were best friends too.

"Why do you smoke that stuff?" I whispered. "It's disgusting."

She just shrugged while I shoved her towards the bathroom. "Brush

1

your teeth or use mouthwash or something. Dad needs to talk to us. And don't forget to change your clothes!" I rolled my eyes thinking that she was busted this time for sure.

A couple minutes later, Rena was ready. We walked downstairs, dreading whatever Dad had to say. He heard us coming and was waiting at the bottom of the staircase.

"Come into my office, girls." Uh oh. Dad sounded serious and stressed out, but also nervous. What had happened this time? I looked questioningly at my sister. From her confused expression I knew that she was just as clueless as I was.

We walked in and sat down in the twin leather chairs across from his large mahogany desk, just staring at each other for a moment, waiting for my Dad to say something.

My father was a handsome man. He had short, jet black hair, and bright blue eyes. He was about 6'4 and very muscular. I had his eyes, and was strong just like him. We were so much alike in so many ways. My black hair was shoulder length and the exact shade of his.

Rena looked exactly like our mom did, with long red hair down to her waist and bright green eyes. We were total opposites, and no one ever believed that we were sisters.

My father usually had a sweet, pleasant face, but at the time, it was lined with stress. I hated the look on it. The easy, joking features that were usually there were completely gone.

"What's wrong, Dad?" I asked, "Did someone die or something?"

"No... Well, yes, but I'll get to that in a minute." He paused for a moment, as if he was thinking about how he should continue. When he finally spoke, I wished that he hadn't.

"I've chosen your mates. The pack needs to expand and this is the only way." His voice was completely devoid of emotion.

Rena and I just stared at him in total shock. When my father said "pack" he meant our werewolf pack. We were werewolves. My father was the alpha of our pack, and since we were his daughters, he got to choose who we marry. That was the only way to ensure that we expanded the pack with the strongest wolves possible. This all sounds like it's from the Romeo and Juliet era or something, but for the only female daughters of an alpha werewolf, it's just the reality of our life.

"You're joking, right?" Rena asked, incredulously.

"I'm sorry, but no, this isn't a joke. The mates that have been chosen are the Krate brothers of the Nevada Pack."

We were the California pack, and because we were such a large, and powerful pack, Rena and I were highly sot after.

"The Nevada alpha just died a few days ago from a heart attack. Since his sons aren't yet 21, they can't run their pack, so they have to combine with another. They specifically asked for you two. Do you know how much of an honor that is to our family?"

"No!" I shouted, standing up and slamming my hands on his desk. "Nevada is the pack who killed our family and took Mom away from us! Besides that, they're total losers and we're too young to get married! How the hell would marrying murderers give our family honor? I won't do it!" I stormed out of the room, slamming the door behind me. I ran upstairs into my room, and slammed the door before locking it. I knew my reaction was extremely immature and childish, but I didn't care. I sat on my bed trying to think of what to do. I had to figure a way out of this situation. The anger I felt made it hard to hold myself together.

There was no way out of it. I would be forced to marry one of them. The only thing I could do to prevent getting married to one of those idiots was to run away.

-X-

Rena

"I won't do it!" Serenity shouted at our father before storming out of the room, slamming both the door of the study and, after she stomped up the stairs, her bedroom door. I stayed where I was, planning to give Dad a piece of my mind for the first time in years. When Mom died, Serenity was a wreck. She was almost as zombie-like as Dad until she started acting out to vent her emotions. She was just now getting better. How could he put her, us, through another tragedy?

My plan fell through when I looked up at my father, whose head was in his hands.

"Oh Serena, I have no idea what to do without you."

It took me a moment to realize that he was crying. Dad hadn't been even close to the person he was with Mom. He never talked to his friends anymore, he only went to pack meetings and made council decisions. Other than that, he mostly just sulked around the house, taking in nothing and giving nothing back.

Flashback

It had been about a year after Mom's death and Serenity was out on one of her late night rides. She would probably come home smelling like alcohol again. I was surprised Dad never noticed, but then again, he never noticed my pot either. He didn't notice much of anything. It's like when Mom died, Dad's soul went with her.

It was well known that wolves mate for life. It was hard for our kind to accept the death of a loved one, especially a mate. My father looked like a ghost as he walked through the house from day to day. He mostly avoided Serenity and I, but mainly me. I knew that I looked like Mom, but it hurt when Dad looked away from me.

I was sitting on the stairs when I saw Dad. The moonlight shone through a window above the stairs and landed on me. Dad looked up and I could see his unshaven face. His eyes were red and swollen, his hair was uncombed, and his chin quivered like a child's.

"Oh Serena, I miss you so much." He walked up the stairs towards me, and when he reached me, he began to cry as he hugged me. "I don't know what to do without you. Why did you have to die? I need you. I need you so bad."

I did the only thing I could.

"It's alright Brad. I know you and the girls will be fine. I miss you too sweetheart." The words felt so awkward coming out of my mouth, but I couldn't stand to see more heartbreak on his features if he really realized who I was. I rubbed his back as he cried, and when he was finished, I helped him up the stairs and into his bed. I lay down beside him until he fell asleep, and then went to my room. I cried and prayed that things would get better.

End Flashback

Dad still saw me as a reminder of my mother. Seeing the state he was in, I decided it was best to just leave. Quietly, I got up and left, closing the door softly. I walked up to my room and went in. I didn't want to get married but I couldn't think of a way out of it. I thought of my sister and, like she had read my mind, my cell phone rang.

Serenity

I called Rena's cell phone and told her what I was planning. She decided to come with me, because she didn't want to get married any more than I did. I told her to start packing and hung up.

I walked to my closet retrieving two duffel bags. I filled one with as much clothing as I could possibly fit. I went to my desk, and taped under it was a manila envelope with emergency money. I had saved up about $20,000, which seems like a lot, but we are a very wealthy family so it hadn't taken me that long to save. I put the envelope into the other bag and with it, my cell phone, an extra jacket and three of my favorite books. I added my wallet containing my driver's license, $150, a Border's Rewards card, my student ID, and a family picture of my mother, my father, Rena and I from three years ago. Looking at the picture, I had to hold back tears, as it brought back memories of how perfect life was back then.

I grabbed my sleeping bag and a blanket from the back of my closet. I put the blanket in my bag, and then shoved it all under my bed so that if my father came in to check on me like he usually did, he wouldn't see it. I turned my music back on full blast and plopped back onto my bed, opening my book where I left off.

After a few hours, it was 11 PM and I had finished my book. Changing into my pajamas, I laid down and set my alarm clock for 3 AM and slowly drifted off to sleep.

Darkness. Pitch black. I could see nothing. I felt lost, like I would never find my way back to the light. The darkness was suffocating me. I lost all hope, and then the pain came. It pierced right through my center like a cold, steel knife. I tried to scream, to cry, but no sound came.

All of a sudden, a hand reached out of the darkness. I latched onto it with both of mine and was pulled back into the world. I lay flat on my back, gasping for breath and clutching my now painless stomach.

I was in the woods. It was a bright day and the sun was shining directly on me through the trees. The grass was damp and I could hear the chirp of crickets. I whipped my head around as I saw movement in the shadows to my right. A tall, lanky figure stepped towards me. From his thick glasses and nerdy attire, I instantly recognized him as Trevor Krate.

He smiled at me, but the smile wasn't friendly. It was menacing and possessive. He moved his arm from behind his back and in his hand was a long, bloody knife. Looking back at my stomach, I saw blood and the pain started all over again, except this time, I could scream.

I woke gasping for air when my alarm clock went off. I was used to bad dreams by then, but that was the worst yet.

After laying there for a moment to make sure my alarm hadn't woken anyone else, I slowly got out of bed and changed out of my pajamas and into some holey jeans, a T-shirt, and a pair of black high tops. I got the bags out from under my bed and put them by the door. I retrieved my book bag from the closet and put it with the things I was taking with me.

Quietly I opened my door and tip toed across the hall. I opened Rena's door and slipped in. She was still asleep. I went over to her and shook her gently, "Rena, we have to go."

She yawned and slowly got up. When she got up, she stubbed her toe on her night stand and mumbled a curse.

"Maybe it would help if you opened your eyes," I suggested in a whisper. Rolling her eyes at me, she walked to her closet and collected her bags. She whispered a quick prayer before we crept out of the room and silently shut her door. As we passed my room, I grabbed my bags and closed my door. We kept the book bag, but left our other things in the hall way near an open window, and then headed downstairs, careful not to make any noise.

Walking through the hallway, I looked up and admired the portraits hanging on the wall as we passed them. They were of all of the past alphas and their mates that were connected to our family. At the end of the hall hung the perfectly painted portrait of my mother and father. I paused for a moment in front of it and bowed my head to show my respect before continuing to the kitchen.

In our search for some light weight food, we found some chips, a box of crackers, and quite a few cans of beanie weenies. We also got as many bottles of water as my bag could hold. We needed food so that we could hide in the woods for a few days until we could think of some where to go. I put all of the food we found into the empty book bag I got from my closet. I also grabbed a box of plastic forks. When Rena wasn't looking, I slipped a couple bottles of my favorite soda into the bag.

We couldn't use the front door, it squeaked loudly whenever it opened, so we made our way quietly back up stairs to the window where we left our bags. It was the only open window in the house other than the one in our father's room, so we had to exit there. Rena jumped out first. With her perfect werewolf reflexes, she landed on her feet without making a sound. I tossed the bags and sleeping bags out to her. After I threw out the last bag, I got ready to jump, and of course, being my normal klutzy self, I slipped and landed in a crouch.

"Nice," Rena whispered sarcastically.

"Shut up," I whispered back, already irritated.

We quietly sprinted to the detached garage and straight for Rena's black Porsche. She opened the trunk, threw in our stuff, and then closed it. Rena walked to the drivers' side door, opening it quietly.

"Hey Rena," I whispered. "I'm gonna take my motorcycle just in case we need quick transportation." She just nodded and slipped into her car.

My bike was a silver and black Ducati. I had convinced my father to let me get it instead of a car. He wasn't very happy about it at first; he kept showing me pictures of nice cars and dropping hints. He was afraid, and he didn't want me to get hurt, but after he saw how well I road it, he didn't bother me about it anymore.

Since her car's engine was really quiet, she went ahead and started it while I opened the garage door. I made my way to my motorcycle and pushed it out of the garage and down the drive-way. Pausing for a moment, I looked back at our house.

"Goodbye Dad," I whispered, letting a single tear flow down my cheek. "I love you."

Once on the road, Rena followed slowly behind me. When we got far enough down the road that no one in my house would hear the motorcycle, I climbed on, started the bike, and took off into the darkness.

I exited out onto the highway and followed it for a few miles, past the hiking trails that Rena and I hiked every week. There was an opening in the trees just big enough for Rena's car. She slowly drove it through the trees, far enough to where no one would see it in the daylight. I stopped my bike near her car and got off. She opened the trunk again and we took out our bags. I draped my bags across my bike, and with Rena carrying hers and me pushing the bike, we made our way through the woods where we would stay until we could think of a plan.

We walked for several miles through the dense woods. After what felt like hours of walking, we came to an old, rusty barge that was burnt and falling apart. We decided this would be a perfect spot to stay for our time spent in the woods. I put my bike by a tree and grabbed my bags, then jumped up onto the barge. Rena had already climbed up and was looking around.

There were rooms that were still partially intact, but there was glass everywhere, and some holes in the floor. It took a while, but using our shoes, we moved all the glass to one side. We finished faster than humans would have because of our supernatural skills.

Rena had thought to pack a tent, so we put it up in a room to the side and secured it with rocks. After we laid out our sleeping bags and blankets, I walked around, looking for a place to put the food and water. I found some partially burnt shelves on a wall of the barge, and lined up the food and water on them, before I set the book bag against the shelves.

Rena walked off to find fire wood, and probably to smoke. While she was gone, I looked for places on the barge where we could hide if necessary. I found a few good spots and moved the glass out of the way. The entire barge smelled pretty bad, so we didn't need to worry about anyone smelling us.

I was standing at the edge of the barge, looking out at Lake Tahoe when I heard Rena running fast through the woods back toward the barge. I instantly knew something was wrong. I whirled around to face her as she jumped up onto the barge and I could hear her frantic breathing.

"What's wrong?" I asked. But I didn't have to. The wind blew the scent directly into my face.

"Werewolves," she gasped as two men jumped up onto the barge with us.

-X-

Unknown

I was standing in the funeral home, thinking about my plan with a grin on my face. It was completely fool proof. Other than the Noonans, who were being taken care of, no one would ever know. I knew there was no chance of being found out.

"Sir?"

I turned around to see one of the men I hired looking nervously at me. "What do you want?" I snapped.

"Well, sir, they have refused the offer. They are gone."

"What?!" I shouted.

"That's not all. The Noonan boys have escaped."

I was seething by the time he finished his sentence. "You might want to leave now, before I do something that I *won't* regret." He ran off quickly.

A voice came out of the shadows near the front pew. "So what's the plan now?" My brother asked.

I answered after a moment. "We are going to find them. All of them. The Noonans will be killed. And if our offer is refused a second time, all of them will be killed."

Chapter Two

Boys Will Be Wolves

The two werewolves were in human form, and they were definitely male. They looked to be in their late teens, possibly brothers, because both of them had the same black hair. One had short hair, silver looking eyes, and he seemed to be around 6'2. The other, had chin length hair with swooping bangs that covered one of his beautiful hazel eyes, and he was about 6'0. They both had book bags on their backs.

I took in the situation in about a second, and phased so that I could stand in front of Rena. In wolf form, we weren't huge, scary monsters like everyone thinks; we were just like normal wolves. My fur was black, white, and gray, and Rena's was pure white.

I was crouched down and snarling at the men. Rena was standing behind me, frozen in human form from shock and fear. The boy with the short black hair phased into a large, dark brown wolf. The other boy was just standing there with shock and another emotion I couldn't detect covering his face, staring at me.

We were both crouched down and growling at each other. I started to advance toward the other wolf a little, when finally, the other guy spoke.

"Wait!" he exclaimed. "We don't want to hurt you. We need a place to hide. Do you mind if we stay here too, at least for a little while?"

I didn't know whether to trust him or not. I was still growling with my suspicions. Suddenly, Rena grabbed my tail and yanked me backwards. I turned my head and bared my teeth at her, but she wasn't concerned, she knew that I wouldn't hurt her. I huffed and picked up what was left of my clothes in my mouth, and walked to the part of the barge where we had stowed our things. I phased back to human form and inspected what was left of my clothes. My t-shirt was completely ruined, there was no way I could ever wear it again. Thankfully, my favorite jeans were still intact except for a new rip at mid- thigh. I could still wear them. I grabbed a new pair of underwear, t-shirt, and bra, since my previous ones were shredded, and dressed quickly.

When I returned to the group, I saw that the boy with short hair was already in new clothes. They were just waiting for me.

"I guess I believe you," I said. "You can stay here, and I'm sorry for almost ripping you to pieces. We ran away too, and I didn't know why you were here, so I was just being cautious."

"I don't really think you could hurt me," said the guy with the short hair. I rolled my eyes and snorted at his comment. "But it's okay though. I'm Zane and this is my brother Zander."

"Hi," Zander said to me. I smiled at him, and noticed that Rena was staring at Zane.

"I'm Serenity, and this is my sister Rena. I'm sixteen, and Rena's eighteen. How old are you two?" I asked.

"I'm seventeen and Zane is nineteen," Zander said.

"So why did you two run away?" Rena asked them sounding quite curious and, still, staring at Zane.

"We were under the death penalty with our pack. We heard something we shouldn't have, so our family was sentenced to death.

We couldn't save our parents, because we were in jail. They killed our parents, and when they came to open our cell, we fought and ran. We came here because it's far away from them," Zander explained.

"Wow," I said, intrigued, "our problem isn't that bad. I kinda feel like a big baby."

"What happened with you two?" Zander asked. He flipped his hair to the side, and now I could now see both of his gorgeous hazel eyes. He stared at me, curious.

"Well," I started, looking at Rena. She looked back at me with uncertainty for a moment, and then nodded. We didn't want to divulge information that could get us caught.

"Our father is the alpha of the California pack." When they heard this, they looked a little suspicious; like they thought we were going to turn them in. I hurried on before they could jump to conclusions.

"He wanted to expand the pack, so he was going to mate us with the Krate brothers of the Nevada pack. We told him that we wouldn't do it, so I figured out a way for us to escape. I went to my room to pack, called Rena's cell and she agreed. We left last night. We hid Rena's car and walked my motorcycle through the woods until we came across this barge." They looked at each other for a moment, and then just stared at me.

"What? It's not like I have antlers! Stop looking at me like that." Everyone started laughing, and after a moment, I did too.

After we all calmed down, Rena jumped off the barge and walked off into the woods. "Where is she going?" Zane asked.

"Probably to smoke pot," I answered.

Zane looked interested. "Maybe she'll share," he said and then followed after her. Zander just shook his head.

"That is so gross," I said.

"I know, I keep telling him that but he doesn't care." I could tell that Zander was just as disgusted as I was.

I showed Zander where Rena and I were going to sleep.

"Do you have a tent?" I asked.

"No," he answered, "we don't really have anything except for a few pieces of clothing."

"Its okay, our tent is big enough for all four of us." I showed him where I stored the food, and where we could make a fire. After I ran out of things to show him, I got an idea. It was risky, but that's part of what made things fun.

"Do you want to go for a ride on my motorcycle?" I asked him, grinning.

He looked nervous. "As long as you don't crash."

~X~

We walked my motorcycle though the woods until we found a large, grassy clearing. It was huge, the perfect size for riding.

At the edge of the clearing, I got on the bike and patted the seat behind me. Zander looked a little worried, but sighed and got on the bike behind me.

"So how long have you had this bike?"

"About six months." Hearing this made him look a little more worried.

"Please don't crash," he said.

"Don't you trust me?" I asked with a smirk.

"Not really."

"Don't be such a baby," I said as I started the bike. "You better hold on tight." Then we were moving. I didn't go too fast yet, I didn't want to freak him out, so I gradually increased our speed.

It was a pretty big clearing, probably about half a mile in diameter, surrounded by miles and miles of trees.

"Woo!" Zander yelled. I could tell that he liked it.

Zander seemed like an okay guy. I was kind of glad that he and

Zane had found us. It would have sucked for me to be alone, stuck with just Rena to keep me company. As long as she had her pot, she'd be fine, but I knew that she would like having them around too.

I finally stopped the bike and we got off. When I looked at him, he had a huge grin spread across his face.

"That was awesome," he exclaimed. "I haven't had that much fun in a while. Thank you, Serenity." He looked into my eyes, and my heart skipped a beat. I knew he noticed, too, because he smirked back at me.

"You're welcome," I mumbled. We stood there for a moment, just looking at each other. Finally, I spoke first. "We should get back. Rena and Zane are probably getting worried." I broke our gaze and started pushing the bike back the way we came.

-X-

Rena

"What? It's not like I have antlers! Stop looking at me like that!" Everyone started laughing at Serenity's joke.

After a moment, I walked to the side of the barge and jumped down, heading into the woods. Though I would never recommend it, smoking was my way to relieve stress and forget my problems. Most of my problems and bad history I kept to myself. I didn't want to burden anyone or make them as miserable as I truthfully was. I felt that I needed to keep a strong front for Serenity.

It was about two minutes before I noticed that I was being followed. I spun around to see Zane coming up behind me.

"Oh. It's just you." I waited for him to catch up and then fell into step beside him. I felt around in the pocket of my shorts for the joint that I had stashed there, hoping it hadn't broken. Thankfully, it was still intact as I placed it between my lips and used my lighter to light it. Inhaling, I looked over at Zane. His eyes followed my joint as I pulled it away from my mouth to exhale. I smiled as I held it out to him. "You wanna hit it?"

He offered me a grateful smile as he took it. "All of this runaway stuff has me so stressed out. I really needed that. Thanks Rena," he said as he handed it back.

"I know what you mean." Strangely, I didn't feel uncomfortable as I walked with Zane like I did around other guys. Lowering my voice to a murmur, I offered my condolences. "I'm sorry about your parents."

Zane shrugged, but I could see the sadness in his eyes. "I'm not gonna say that I don't miss them or anything, 'cause I do. I really am extremely upset. But we just weren't that close. They were always off on business. Zander and I saw them maybe twenty minutes a week, tops."

I was shocked. My father may not have been very responsive, but at least he was there. My thoughts were cut short when I heard the rumble of Serenity's motorcycle about half a mile away.

"Sounds like Serenity is showing off," I said with a smile, trying to lighten the mood. He chuckled.

"Did you see the way Zander was looking at her? I've never seen him look at anyone like that. It was like he was seeing the sun for the first time."

"Yeah, I noticed," I answered as I heard Zander "wooing" in the distance. All of a sudden, I detected a slightly different smell of marijuana than the joint I had just put out. It wasn't smoky, but fresh. "No way," I said as it registered in my brain. A grin spread across my face as I sniffed the air and then took off running forward.

"What is it?" Zane called, running behind me. I stopped in front of some large bushes of the five leaved plant I so relied on. Zane stopped beside me with a look of awe on his face. With the small jolt of excitement we just received, we started laughing as we grabbed as much of the buds as we could.

-X-

Serenity

When we arrived back at the barge, I knew I shouldn't have worried. Zane and Rena were stoned out of their minds. Rena ran up to me, giggling.

"Guess what?!" she asked me, still laughing.

"What?"

"We found a whole field full of weed!" She grinned and started bouncing around. Most of the times I had seen someone high, it relaxed them and made them calm. Sometimes they would even fall asleep. Marijuana seemed to have a completely opposite effect on my sister. She turns hyper and starts bouncing off the walls.

"Calm down," I told her. "Go ogle at Zane or something." She rolled her eyes and skipped back to Zane. They started talking again, effectively ignoring Zander and me.

"Well that was weird," Zander said. When I looked at him, he flipped his hair out of his eyes and smiled at me.

"Are you hungry?" I asked him.

"Yeah, I am. We might want to find some food before Zane and Rena get the munchies." We both laughed. We walked across the main part of the barge, being careful where we stepped. I pointed at the shelves.

"What do you want?" I asked him.

"It doesn't matter," he replied. "I'll eat whatever you eat."

"Chips?" He nodded.

I grabbed the bag off the partially burnt shelf. We then walked to the tent and went inside, it was definitely getting cold. We sat down on my sleeping bag, and we talked the entire time that we were eating. We talked about everything, about books, movies, family, friends, everything. We both liked a lot of the same things, and we were so much alike. He laughed when I told him that I could sit and watch a million scary movies and be fine, but then jump or shriek, scaring the hell out of myself when someone knocks on the door or when my cell phone goes off.

After we were finished with the chips, I brought out the two bottles of soda that I had hidden from Rena in my bag. I handed one to Zander, "this is the only soda I have, and I managed to hide it from Rena. We have plenty of water, though."

He chuckled. "Thanks, it's my favorite."

"Mine too," I laughed.

We sat in silence looking at each other, drinking our soda. "What are you thinking about?" he asked me.

"Nothing, but yet everything. This entire screwed up situation. What are you thinking about?"

"I'm thinking about how beautiful your eyes are," he said. "They are such a beautiful blue." His unexpected statement made me blush.

"Your eyes are pretty amazing, too. I've always liked hazel eyes."

"You think my eyes are amazing?" He questioned.

"Yes." He smiled at me, and it made me feel warm inside.

He continued smiling, and oh my God, he had such a gorgeous smile. That was my last thought before I heard Rena's howl pierce through the silence.

~X~

Unknown

After I was calm again, I sent for another one of my men. When he appeared at my side, he seemed to be a little frightened. I smiled to myself, loving the effect I had on people.

"Have they been found yet?" I asked him.

"No, sir, but their scent has been detected in California. I have five of our best wolves tracking them. They should be in our custody again within the next few hours."

"Good. Make sure of it. Or else *you* will pay the price."

"Yes, sir."

My fool proof plan seemed to have a few holes, but they were being patched up. I wasn't going to lose this fight. Too much depended on it. We were in way to deep to just stop now.

CHAPTER THREE

The Fur Will Fly

When I heard Rena's howl, I rushed out of the tent with Zander right on my heels. We ran to the main part of the barge, and saw that Zane and Rena both had phased into wolf form. They were staring into the woods, growling. I was confused until I saw five wolves coming out of the trees.

Just wonderful, I thought, right before phasing into wolf form. Zander phased right after me, and I noticed that his fur was completely black.

I knew that Rena wasn't the best fighter, especially while high, so I stepped in front of her to protect her from the immanent attack. The other wolves began growling and baring their teeth as they stalked toward us. We backed up some so that we could fight on the barge and not in the woods. Then they jumped up onto the barge and tried to surround us.

I could tell when they were going to attack right before they did. I shoved Rena out of the way as a white wolf lunged at her. When it hit me, it bit into my hind leg. I turned my head and bit its ear and pulling until it unlatched its teeth. As soon as it let go, another wolf started its attack on me. Out of everyone there, of course I would be the one to get tag-teamed. I threw off a brown wolf as the white one tried to bite at my throat. My hind leg was hurting pretty badly from where it tried to take a chunk out of it only a moment ago.

Rena, thank god, was fighting the smallest wolf and was doing really well. Zander seemed to be unharmed as well; he was fighting a gray wolf about the size of the one's I was fighting. Zane was fighting the largest wolf, and he seemed to be having a little bit of trouble, but I was confident that he wouldn't lose.

I had just grabbed the back of the white wolf's neck and ripped it away from my throat when the brown wolf jumped back onto my back. Yelping in pain, I let go of the white wolf and tried to get the brown wolf off of me, but it was latched to my back with both its teeth and claws. The white wolf lunged for my throat again and I jumped out of the way, and rolled over onto my back to try to get the other wolf off. When it still didn't let go, I ran off the barge and threw myself against a tree. The wolf finally unlatched its teeth and fell off of my back. I turned and immediately lunged at it. We rolled for a few moments, both of us trying to get the advantage. When I finally had the chance, I latched my teeth around its neck. I jerked my head to the side and I heard the wolf's neck break. I let go of it and it fell limp to the ground.

I felt bad for killing it, but only for a moment because the white wolf had grabbed my hind leg again. I threw the leg back and hit it in the face. As I turned towards it, it grabbed part of my back and threw me back against the tree. Momentarily dazed, all I could hear around me was snarling and the snapping of jaws. After my head cleared, I looked over to see the white wolf running towards me. At the last second, I rolled out of the way, which was excruciating. It slammed head first into the tree and I jumped on top of it. I was disgusted as I ripped its throat out, the hot, salty blood flooding my mouth and throat.

After coughing up as much of the blood as I could, I limped back to the barge and jumped up to see if anyone needed my help. Werewolves in close range can open their minds to each other so they can communicate in wolf form. Zander and Rena were just finishing off their wolves, but Zane was still fighting pretty hard.

"Zane," I sent telepathically. "Do you need any help?"

"A little," he shot back.

I ran over to him and grabbed the wolf's hind leg. I pulled hard on it to distract the wolf, effectively making it snap towards me .As soon as its attention was averted to me, Zane reached and grabbed it by the throat. Now that he had it under control, I let go and watched as he killed it.

Once I saw that everyone was okay, I went to the room with my clothes and the tent. I phased so I could look through my bag. Once I found some clothes, I dressed quickly so that I could get rid of the bodies. I walked back to the main part of the barge, and without saying a word to anyone, I jumped off the side and limped my way to the bodies that had now reverted back into human form.

The white wolf turned out to be a man with platinum blond hair. The brown wolf was a brunette man. They were both very muscular, so I was a little bit proud of myself for being able to take them both at once.

I grabbed the feet of the blond man and started to drag it far into the woods so we wouldn't have to look at them. I walked back to the other body and dragged him to the same spot, hoping that we wouldn't be having anymore company any time soon. Rena, Zane, and Zander were all back in human form and dragging the bodies of the other wolves as well.

"I'll be right back," I told them. I walked back to the barge. Looking around, I saw the container of half evaporated gasoline that I had noticed earlier. I grabbed it and walked back to the pile of bodies. I poured some of the gas over the heap and said, "Rena, give me your matches." She tossed me a little red package with a heart sticker on it.

I had picked a spot that didn't have a lot of grass so I wouldn't catch everything on fire. I pulled out a match and lit it, throwing it onto the bodies. After a second, they burst into flames. I tossed the matches back to Rena. "Can you keep this controlled?" I asked them. "I don't want to burn down the whole forest." Rena nodded her head and looked at me with eyes full of worry. I just ignored it and walked off. About half mile from where I started, I stopped at the edge of the lake. I sat by it for a while, thinking and trying to clean myself up a little. Finally, when I couldn't take it anymore, I broke down and started to cry.

CHAPTER FOUR

Pot Heads and First Aid

I know what you're thinking. If you had to kill someone to defend yourself, why would you feel bad? Well, if you actually kill someone, no matter what the reason, if you have a heart, you will feel bad. I had just killed two people. When we ran away, the thought that something like this would ever happen never crossed my mind. When we met Zander and Zane, I figured that we would inevitably have to fight someone. They were wanted dead, so of course, someone would be looking for them. Now that we were positive that there were people still after them, we couldn't leave them to fend for themselves. If Rena and I wouldn't have been there, Zander and Zane most likely would be dead.

That wasn't the only reason I was upset. My entire life had been uprooted. It would never be the same again. I didn't know when would be my next chance to see my family and friends. I didn't know if I would even get a chance.

If we went back, I would have to marry into the Krate family, the family that had already ruined my life once before when they killed half my family. Now they had the nerve to do it again. They better hope they never find me, unless they had a death wish.

I knew we couldn't stay at the barge any longer. If they could find us once, they could find us again. We would probably have to leave early tomorrow. We would need to go to a big city somewhere, preferably far away. I had a friend who made fake IDs, passports, birth certificates, everything we would ever need to start a new life. We could go back to high school so we could actually get diplomas and maybe we could even go to college at some point.

When Zander and I were talking earlier, he was telling me that they were from the Washington pack. I was thinking about possible places to go when I heard leaves crunching from behind me. I turned around, ready to phase in an instant, when Zander stepped out of the trees.

"Oh, thank God it's just you," I said, and sat back down. Zander walked over and sat down beside me.

"Are you okay?" he asked.

"Yeah, I'm fine."

"Are you sure? Because... I mean, you look beautiful and all... but you don't look so good right this minute. You look like you were hurt pretty bad."

"I can't really feel anything. Are you okay?"

"Yep," he smiled a little, "not a scratch on me."

"I wouldn't have been this bad if I wouldn't have had to fight two wolves at once. But I'm kinda proud of myself for still being alive."

"Yeah, I'm really glad that you're alive, too. But maybe we should get back to the barge so we can clean your wounds and see how bad they are."

"Okay."

Zander helped me up and we started walking. He saw me limping and glanced down at my blood soaked shoe. He was instantly worried. Before I knew what was happening, he had scooped me up into his arms and was carrying me.

"What are you doing?" I asked, shocked. "I can walk, you know."

"I can see you limping. It hurts every time you take a step."

"I can deal with it. You don't have to carry me." He looked into my eyes.

"But I want to." He smiled at me.

"Fine," I mumbled. He carried me back to the barge and past Rena and Zane. Of course they were staring. They both had half smiles as they saw me pouting and Zander smirking. A moment later, they realized why he was carrying me and followed with worried looks.

He carried me to the area where we kept the food and water. "Rena, go get a blanket," Zander said. Rena hurried to the tent. She brought back a blanket and another T-shirt for me.

"Why did you get another shirt? What's wrong with this one? I just changed it."

"Um, Serenity, the back of your shirt is covered in blood."

"Oh," was all I could say as Rena spread the blanket on the floor. Zander gently set me down on the blanket and then moved to sit in front of me.

Carefully, he pulled off my shoe and sock. He smiled when he saw the black polish on my toenails that matched my finger nails.

"You wouldn't happen to have a towel by any chance?" He asked as he looked up at me. I shook my head. He then grabbed the bottle of water that Zane was holding out to him, opened it and poured a little on the dirty bite on my ankle. He quickly pulled off his shirt and pressed it against my ankle. I barely noticed the pain, because all of my attention was focused on his bare chest. He was very muscular and had the most amazing six pack that I had ever seen in my life. I was close to drooling when Rena cleared her throat. I unwillingly looked up at her, and she rolled her eyes at me and began to speak.

"So where are we gonna go? We can't stay here because when those other wolves don't return to whoever sent them, someone will come looking for them."

"We will probably need to go east somewhere, unless we go to Alaska or Hawaii, but I think that Alaska seems a little cold, even for our high body temperatures. And to get to Hawaii, we would need to get on a plane, but we wouldn't have the time to get fake IDs," Zane said.

"So I guess somewhere east is our only option right now," Zander said. "If that's okay with you girls."

"Fine with me," I said.

"Me too," Rena agreed.

After Zander finished cleaning the bite, we found out that it wasn't as bad as it seemed, but it would heal better if we could get to a hospital and get stitches.

At this point, Rena's half dead brain cells decided to work.

"Hey!" she said, "I forgot that I packed a first aid kit!"

I turned and gave her the death glare. "Great timing, Rena," I said to her sarcastically. She just shrugged as she walked off to get it. When she came back, she handed the kit to Zander. He opened it and rifled through it, seeing what all was there. He took out some peroxide, a roll of gauze, and some medical tape.

The bite on my ankle was still bleeding, so he carefully pressed his shirt to it again to wipe off the blood. Since I wasn't as distracted by his chest at that moment, I hissed a little at the throbbing pain I had previously been ignoring. He looked up and gave me a small apologetic smile. I could tell that he hated doing anything that hurt me. After pouring some peroxide on it, he applied some antibiotic ointment. He then took the gauze and quickly wrapped some around my ankle and secured it with the tape.

When he finished, he looked at me awkwardly. "Um," he said, blushing. "I'll let Rena take care of your back and neck. Zane and I will wait in the other room." I nodded and they got up and walked out.

Rena sat down behind me while I carefully pulled my shirt off and sat it beside me. I was definitely feeling the pain now.

"Uh, Serenity, this looks really bad... I don't think I can do this." Rena put her hand over her mouth and rushed out of the room. I picked up my t-shirt and covered my chest. I could hear Rena talking to Zander in the other room. "I just can't do it, Zander. I can't stand the sight of blood. I mean... a little, like what was on her ankle was okay, but that... I can't. You'll have to do it."

I sighed. "Its okay, I'll be fine," I shouted. "Don't worry about it." I started to put my shirt back on as Zander walked in.

"Do you really think that I would let you sit here in pain? Your back could get infected. I don't even want to know where the mouths of those wolves have been." He sat down behind me. "Whoa," he said. "This does seem pretty bad. There are at least four bite marks on your back and a few on the back of your neck. This is probably gonna hurt a bit." I could tell he was still embarrassed, but I liked that he was such a gentleman.

He took the bottle of water and poured some on a clean area of his shirt. He dabbed at the wounds, trying to make sure that he cleaned them thoroughly. I clenched my teeth together tightly so I wouldn't scream. The pain was excruciating. I couldn't believe that I hadn't felt it before. Zander finished cleaning it with peroxide and put on some antibiotic ointment.

"Uh," he hesitated, "I need to wrap some gauze around it to keep it clean."

I understood what he was trying to say. I sat up straight and dropped my shirt, embarrassing us both. He put his arms around me and started wrapping gauze around, securing it with more medical tape. He finished up his work by putting a couple big bandages on my neck. I started to reach for my new shirt and gasped when the motion strained my back a little. He reached over grabbing the shirt for me, and helped me put it on so I wouldn't have to move my back muscles as much.

"Thanks," I mumbled. He helped me up and into the other room with Rena and Zane. "Did you puke?" I asked Rena, and laughed a little at her weak stomach.

"Nope, I just needed to get away from the blood." Rena said.

We walked over and sat down.

"So where are we gonna go?" I asked

"We could go to Colorado," Zander suggested.

"We should go farther east than that," Zane argued.

"Well what about Virginia? There isn't much farther east in the country than that," I said.

"Other than the ocean," Rena added, being an ass. Zander and I just looked at her. "What?" she asked.

We ignored her, "I think that's a good idea, Serenity," Zander said.

"I agree," Zane said.

We all went to bed after that, planning to pack up and leave early tomorrow.

-X-

Unknown

I threw the glass that I was drinking from and it shattered against the wall in the exact spot his head was only seconds ago.

"What?!"

"I'm sorry, sir! The men I sent aren't responding. Every time I call it goes straight to voice mail."

"Well go look for them! I want the Noonans found! And I mean *now*."

"Yes, sir." The man ran out of the room.

"How hard is it to find two teenage boys?" I yelled.

"Apparently, very hard," my annoying brother retorted.

"You know what? If you are going to be so negative, why don't *you* go find them? Or better yet, go jump off a roof. Then I'll never have to listen to your stupid voice again."

He laughed. "You know as well as I do that it wouldn't kill me."

"Yeah, I know. But sometimes I wish it would."

CHAPTER FIVE

Phone Call

When I woke up, everyone was still asleep. I got out of the tent and went to retrieve my cell phone out of my bag. I looked through the contacts list until I found Damien's name. He was the only friend that I knew could make the fake documents that we would need. He lived in Virginia, so that could give us a lot of help. I walked out of hearing range and called him. After listening to about half of his call tone, he answered.

"Serenity! Where are you? Samantha called me and said that you and Rena were missing!" Samantha was a friend of mine in our pack.

"Relax, I'm fine, but I'm not going home. I need a favor. I'm gonna need four IDs, birth certificates, and passports. Can you do that?"

"Sure I can do that. But what's going on?"

"My father mated me and Rena. I'm definitely not getting married any time soon, especially not with one of the Krate brothers."

"Ew... now I understand why you ran away. I guess I can get you the documents, as long as you keep in touch with me so I know that you're safe."

Damien had been my best friend since we were five. His parents died when he was 15 and now he and his sister, Danni, lived with their Aunt. They were also werewolves, so when they had to move, they had to join the Virginia pack.

"I will, and I'll see you soon. We're coming your way so I'll give you the details later, okay?"

"Okay."

"And Damien?"

"Yeah?"

"If you tell any one that we're coming, and I mean anyone, I will tear you to shreds. You know I can."

He laughed. "Yeah I know, I won't say anything to anyone."

"Good. Bye Damey. Love you."

"Love you too. Bye Ren."

I hung up the phone, and by this time Rena was up, out of the tent and walking towards me.

"Were you calling someone? You know that they can trace calls."

"Damien wouldn't trace my call. I went ahead and told him that we are going to need IDs and stuff."

"Okay," Rena said. "That's good. What time is it?"

"Around noon, so we should probably wake up Zane and Zander. We need to get every thing figured out so we can leave." Rena walked back towards the tent to wake them up. I went over to the shelf where I stored the food and started to pack it back into the book bag I had brought it in. I left out four cans of beanie weenies and four bottles of water for breakfast. I zipped everything up and set it back down. I juggled the food to the main part of the barge where everyone was sitting on a blanket waiting for me. Once Zander saw me he hurried over to help me with the food.

We sat the food down and every one grabbed a can. While we were eating, we discussed Damien and our means of transportation, school, and living accommodations. Once we got to Virginia, we were going to find a place to stay at until we had IDs to rent an apartment or house. After that we would enroll in school and get jobs.

We finished eating and set our trash aside. We packed up all of our stuff and the tent. Once we were finished, Zander helped me push my motorcycle through the woods. After a few hours, we were back to Rena's car. We put all of the bags into the car and grabbed mine and Rena's motorcycle helmets that we kept in her car for when I took her places. I gave her's to Zander and I put mine on. Rena and Zane got into her car as Zander and I climbed onto my bike. We pulled out onto the high way once we couldn't hear any cars. We were finally on our way out of California following Rena's GPS.

Of all places to stop for lunch, we stopped in Reno, Nevada. Rena and I were paranoid and kept looking over our shoulders. But strangely, Zander and Zane seemed to be more paranoid than Rena and I were. I had a feeling that there was something that they weren't telling us. But I let it go for the time being. We were all getting hungry, so we decided on a strip of fast food restaurants. Rena and Zane went to Wendy's and Zander and I decided to go to Taco Bell. There were only a few other people in the restaurant, so once we got our food, we moved to the back, sitting in an empty booth.

"We need to get a truck or something so we don't have to ride my motorcycle all the way to Virginia," I said, thinking about how sore we would be if that was the case.

"Yeah that would probably be a good idea, but how are we supposed to get enough money for that?"

"Zander... I have money. I have like $20,000 dollars," Zander looked shocked. "I've saved money since I was like ten years old. I usually only buy books and clothes. And I don't shop a lot like a lot of other girls. I just phase so often that I ruin a lot of clothes."

"Wow... well I have like, no money... at all."

I smiled at him, thinking about how cute he was when he was shocked.

"I know. That's why I paid for your food. It doesn't matter to me though. Rena has money, too, so even if I buy a truck, we'll still have enough money to live on for a while. When we get to Virginia and get our IDs and stuff, I'm going to get a job. I really want to go back to high school, too, so I can actually do something with my life later on. What are you going to do?"

"I'll definitely do the same. I don't know exactly what I want to be, but I know that I want to go to college."

"I do, too. We are either going to have to work really hard and get some type of scholarships or get really good jobs," I laughed.

Zander smiled comfortingly back at me.

We ate in silence for a few minutes, and then Zander looked at me thoughtfully.

"Serenity... do you want to go out on a date with me? Right now wouldn't exactly count since you paid, but I'd like to take you out somewhere nice." He looked nervous, like he was really worried that I would say no.

I smiled at him. "Yes, of course I will. I really would like to go out with you." He looked as excited as I felt.

We finished eating and walked outside. On the other side of the street were houses. Sitting in a driveway like it was meant for us, I saw a sign about a black, 2007 Ford F150 for sale for only $6,000.00.

I stopped walking and my mouth dropped. Zander stopped too and turned around and looked at me.

"What's wrong?" he asked. I just smiled and pointed across the street. He turned and looked. "Wow... how's that for good luck?" he laughed. "Do you want that one?"

"Yeah I do, but I don't know anything about cars, so if there was something wrong with it, I wouldn't know."

"That's okay, Zane and I will go take a look at it, and we're pretty good with trucks."

Just then I had my first extremely girly moment, I squealed and hugged him.

"Thank you Zander! I always wanted a truck!"

Zander laughed and hugged me back. "Well if you're this excited, let's go look at it."

"Okay," I said, still smiling. "I need to text Rena first so she doesn't freak out."

After I texted her, we walked over to my bike. There weren't any cars coming, so we pushed my bike across the street towards the truck.

I walked up to the front door and knocked, anxiously hoping that someone was home. A man who looked to be in his early twenties answered.

"Hi," I said. "I want to take a look at your truck." Zander was over by my bike, leaning against it. The man glanced over my shoulder at him and then looked back at me. He was kind of handsome, with dark brown hair and brown eyes, and wasn't quite as tall as Zander.

"Okay," he said smiling at me. "If you want to go ahead and look at it while I go and get the title and the keys, it's unlocked." I nodded and went over to the truck. Waving Zander over, I opened the driver's side door and got in to check it out, while Zander climbed in the passenger side. There was a brand new radio with a CD player installed, and the inside of the truck was in perfect condition. Zander was leaning over the seat and checking out the back seats when the man came out of his house again. I popped the hood and we both hopped out.

"While I talk to him, you go ahead and check out the engine and stuff. Zane and Rena are walking across the street right now, so he can help." Zander nodded, propping the hood and started poking around the engine.

I walked over to the man. "So the price is $6,000.00 right?" I asked, as Rena walked up and handed me my wallet.

"Yeah, my name is Ryan, by the way. And you are?"

I smiled at him, "my name is Tabetha and this is my sister, Monica," I told him, giving him random names. I didn't want anyone to be able to trace us. "That is Dustin," I told him pointing to Zander, "and Bobby." I pointed at Zane, giving them the first names that popped into my head. I made sure to say it loud enough for them to hear me.

"Hey, Dustin," I called to Zander. He looked back at me. "How does it look?"

"Perfect, there's absolutely nothing wrong with it." He looked a little confused at the use of a fake name.

"If there's nothing wrong with it, why are you selling it so cheap?" I asked.

"I've been trying to sell it for a couple years now, and no one bought it, so I just kept lowering the price." I nodded; clearly he was just ready to get rid of it.

"Now, if you still want the truck, all I have to do is sign the title over to you and get the money."

I felt so stupid. I should have realized that I couldn't sign a truck title with my real name.

"How about we make a deal?" I put on a flirtatious smile. "If you go ahead and sign the truck over to me, without me signing yet, no questions asked, I'll give you an extra $3,000.00, that way you'll get more money, and I'll get my truck" Ryan was hesitant at first, but in the end I convinced him to sign it without my signature.

Ryan offered to help us get my bike into the truck bed, but I told him that it wouldn't be necessary. He was shocked when Zander picked the bike up himself and put it into the truck. After I paid him the $9,000, Rena and Zane went back across the road, and got into Rena's car. Zander and I got into my new truck, me driving, and followed Rena and Zane back to the interstate. Once we were on the road again, Zander let out a huge laugh. He thought it was so hilarious that I had to flirt with Ryan to get the truck. I thought it was kind of embarrassing. Rena had sent Zander a text message. Apparently, she and Zane also thought it was pretty hilarious. I knew that Rena was most likely looking for my reaction in her rear view mirror, so I gave her a rude hand gesture, which just made Zander laugh harder.

This was going to be a long drive, I thought, rolling my eyes.

CHAPTER SIX

Road Trip

Zander and I took turns driving so that we wouldn't have to stop at a hotel. He liked the truck as much as I did, so we made a deal. Well, we didn't exactly make a deal, I knew that Zander liked the truck, so I told him that he could drive it whenever he wanted, and that we would share it. The truck would be half mine and half his, so he would sign the title too. We argued about it for a while. He didn't want to partially own the truck without paying for his half. We decided that after he got a job, he would give me $4,500 as soon as he had saved enough. I didn't want him to give me his money, but he insisted, so I insisted that until he gave me the money, the truck would still be half his, even without him paying me. We argued about that for a while, until he finally gave in.

We sat in silence for a little while after that. It wasn't an uncomfortable silence; we just sat there, him driving. I was thinking about all of the stuff going on in our lives. I had just started thinking about Zander doctoring my ankle, and staring at his gorgeous abs, when he finally broke the silence.

"So this Damien guy we are going to see, he's your best friend, right?"

"Yes," I answered. "We have been best friends since we were little. His parents died when he was 15, so he and his little sister, Danni, had to move in with his aunt in Virginia. They're wolves, too, so when they moved, they had to join the Virginia pack."

Zander nodded. "So did you two ever date?" he asked me, hesitantly. I couldn't help my reaction and I burst out laughing. It was a good thing he was driving. I probably would have run us off the road from how hard I was laughing. Zander just glanced over at me, amused.

"What's so funny?" he asked.

I got myself under control a little. "What's a nice way to put this...? Zander, Damien doesn't really like girls. I don't think he ever has. I think he would be more interested in you than me." I laughed again, and Zander looked relived. Hmm. Was someone a little jealous? I wondered.

"He's not gonna hit on me, is he?" Zander asked, teasing.

"Hmm, maybe," I joked. "You are pretty good looking. Maybe you better watch your back." I started laughing again and he laughed with me. It felt good to finally have something to laugh and smile about.

~X~

Three Days Later

We finally made it to Virginia after a long, four day drive. Zander was driving our truck, and Zane was driving Rena's car, so I took the opportunity to text Rena.

U rnt sleeping r u?

No y?

We need 2 have sum fun after all this driving. Let's go 2 the beach.

I don't have my bathing suit with me.

Then it looks like we r going 2 the mall 1ˢᵗ.

K. I'll tell Zane and change the GPS. R u gonna call Damien and have him meet us @ the beach since he lives right by it?

Yep. How much longer til we get there?

The nearest mall is bout 15 mins away, so after that about an hour.

We r really that close?

Yep.

I'll go ahead and call Damien then and tell him to meet us @ the beach in about 3 hrs.

K. ttyl

"We're going to the mall so Rena can get a bathing suit. We thought going to the beach would be fun," I said to Zander, full of excitement on the prospect of getting out of this truck. He looked excited too.

"Do you and Zane need swim trunks?"

"Yeah. We don't have any with us."

"Okay, I'm gonna tell Damien to meet us at the beach." I called him immediately. He was excited that we were so close, but sad that we were going to the mall without him. He said that he would meet us at the beach, though.

"He's going to bring his boyfriend, Mike, so you don't have to worry about getting hit on," I told Zander, smiling. He just laughed.

Once we got to the mall, we parked and made our way inside the nearest department store. It was still pretty early in the morning, so there weren't many people around yet. Rena and I immediately found two, cute bathing suits. The boys also hadn't taken too long to find swim trunks, so we decided we had enough time to go get some breakfast.

After a huge meal at Bob Evans, we loaded back into our vehicles and made our way towards the beach. It hadn't taken us that long to get there, so we stopped at a rest stop to change.

CHAPTER SEVEN

Surfing and Fist Fights

After we changed into our bathing suits, we met back at my truck. I made sure that Rena put Virginia Beach into the GPS so we wouldn't get lost, then I got into the driver's seat to follow her. Zander got into the passenger seat and Rena and Zane got into Rena's car. We followed Rena for about fifteen minutes and then pulled into a parking lot. We gathered all of our stuff and walked towards the beach.

All of a sudden, by the water, I saw a familiar-looking boy with dark hair. His back was towards me so I took off running towards him, and when I got to him, I jumped on his back.

"Damey!" I yelled.

"Whoa, Ren, calm down! It's just me." He laughed as he stumbled.

I got off his back and he turned around. We hugged each other tightly. "I missed you so much, Damey!" Damien has been my best friend forever.

"I missed you, too, Ren!" We hugged for a moment longer and then Rena, Zane, and Zander reached us.

"Damien, this is Zander," I said pointing to him, "and this is Zane." They all shook hands.

"Nice to meet you," Damien said and the boys both nodded. "This is Mike. Mike, this is Rena and Serenity." He pointed to each of us. Mike had chin length blonde hair and eyes so dark that they looked black. At about 5'10, he was the shortest guy in our group.

After all of the introductions, we hung out on the beach for a little while, just talking and getting to know each other better. After an hour, we decided to go surfing. Zane and Zander didn't know that we could surf, so they challenged us to a surfing contest, thinking that they would win. Damien started to say that I was the best surfer he knew, but I stopped him before he got it out. I put on an innocent smile and said, "What do you think Rena? You want to try and beat these boys?" Rena suddenly realized what I was doing and put on a mischievous smile.

"Hmm," Rena replied. "I think we should try it." She had a hard time not laughing because we surfed all the time in California.

"Okay," I told them. "What happens if we win?" Zander thought it over for a moment.

"How about, when we start school, on the first day the losers have to run through the hall way in only their underwear. And if it's you two, which it probably will be," he said grinning, "only your bras and underwear."

Rena and I were both trying hard not to laugh by now. "It's a deal," I said and we shook hands on it. We walked to a large shack down the beach and rented surfboards and wet suits. Damien and Mike decided not to surf, they were just going to watch and be the judges of who the best surfers were. Damien was laughing because he knew what was going to happen.

"This is gonna be interesting," he mumbled to Mike. I winked at Damien. After we got our wet suits on, we got on our boards and paddled out to wait for some good waves. After a couple minutes, a medium sized wave started coming. Zane took it. He did pretty well. He rode a couple more waves and only fell off the board once. Once he came back, it was Zander's turn. He did a little better than Zane. He rode some bigger waves, but he wiped out twice. He paddled back and smiled, thinking he was really good. I just laughed and told him that he did pretty awesome.

Next it was Rena's turn. She rode a few waves bigger than Zander's and didn't fall once. Zane and Zander started to look a little worried. I just laughed and started to paddle towards a massive wave coming up. "Serenity," Zander called. "Don't you want to try for a smaller one first?" He definitely sounded a little worried now.

"Nope," I called back. As I started to climb the wave, I stood up. I rode it perfectly, not wiping out at all. I rode a few more a little smaller, but the last wave was even bigger than the first. I didn't fall off my board once. As I paddled back to them, Zane and Zander had looks of shock all over their faces. Rena and I just laughed and started back for the beach. When we got there, Zane started questioning us.

"I thought you couldn't surf?" He said.

"We never said that," Rena replied grinning. I was smiling, too.

"But you never said you could," Zander said.

"You didn't ask." I replied as we walked over to Damien and Mike.

"So who are the winners?" Rena asked, smiling because she already knew.

"You and Ren, of course," Damien laughed.

"You could have warned us," Zander said to him.

"I'm sorry, dude. I tried but Ren wouldn't let me. I didn't want to chance it because she would most likely beat me up." I smiled at him.

"Oh Damey, you know I wouldn't do that," I said innocently and laughed. He just rolled his eyes.

After we returned the wet suits and the surf boards, Rena and I decided to lay out for a while and get some sun. We lay on our green and orange towels that we bought to match our bathing suits. All of the guys were down the beach a little ways talking to each other. Rena and I were talking about Zane and Zander. I told her how Zander asked me out on a date. She told me that she and Zane were already dating. We were talking for a little while longer when three guys walked up to us. They all looked to be in their early twenties.

"Hey baby," one of them said to me. The other two were looking back and forth between Rena and me, smiling. "You two wanna come back to our place?"

"No, we would rather stay here, but thanks for the offer," I said, irritated.

"Come on, babe," one of the other guys said. "You'll have fun."

"I can't really think of anything more fun than to hang with you at your place, but sadly, I still have to decline," I told them with major sarcasm. The sun was starting to set, so there weren't many people still at the beach. Damien was whispering to Zane, Zander, and Mike, pointing towards us, and they all turned and looked.

"But here's the thing Hun," the first guy spoke again, "We weren't asking, we were telling."

Rena snorted; she knew they were in for it. I stood up and looked at him. "Are you sure you want to tell me what to do?" I asked him in a pleasant voice.

"Yeah, I'm sure," he answered. "It's not like we are afraid of you two." He smirked at me.

"Well, you should be," I said. He just snorted and grabbed my left arm and pulled me closer to him. He definitely shouldn't have done that...

As one of the other guys started to walk towards Rena, I jerked out of the first guys grip and punched him square in the face so hard he fell backwards. Then I turned and punched the other guy who was just standing there. Rena was getting ready to hit the guy walking towards her. The second guy that I had hit started running because he saw Zander and Zane running swiftly towards us. The first guy I hit had gotten up and grabbed me from behind. I elbowed him in the stomach, and he let go, doubling over. I turned around to face him. I was proud to see that I had broken his nose. Before he could hit me or something worse, Zander had hit him again and pulled me behind him. Zane was going for the guy near Rena. Rena and I watched as Zane and Zander effortlessly beat up the two men. It was actually pretty funny because Zane and Zander weren't even trying very hard. Finally, the men gave up and started running after their friend.

Damien and Mike had already walked over and were sitting with Rena and I. When Zane and Zander sat down with us, Rena and I said thank you, and we all started laughing, thinking the same thing. Those were the stupidest men that had ever walked the Earth.

-X-

Unknown

I was fuming for the next few days. I snapped at almost everyone who talked to me. Finally I got some news. If I had to wait any longer, I'm sure someone would have been hurt.

"Do you want the good news, bad news, or interesting news first?" My brother asked me.

"Just tell me what's going on," I snapped.

"Well, the bad news is that we found traces of a fire near an old barge in California, so they obviously killed our men and burned the bodies. They were no where to be found. The interesting news is that this was found. I thought you would find it interesting. I sure did." He tossed a balled up piece of cloth at me.

"What the hell is this?" I asked as I shook it out. I was a ripped up t-shirt that looked like it belonged to a girl. "How is this good for anything?"

"Smell it and you will find out." I brought the shirt up to my nose and inhaled. My eyes widened.

"They were with the Landon girls?" He nodded.

"The good news is that they were spotted at a beach in Virginia. I just sent men to retrieve them."

"Call them off," I said quickly. "Let them feel safe and get settled in. We will get them when they least expect it." He nodded and left the room.

This was starting to get interesting.

CHAPTER EIGHT

First Kiss

After we finished laughing and making fun of the men that we beat up, Zander and I went for a walk. We were walking down the beach when he suddenly grabbed my hand. I tried to hide my smile but failed. He broke the comfortable silence by asking a question. "So, what's the plan for the living arrangements?" His voice sounded a little worried.

"Well, until Damien can get all of our documents made, we are just going to stay with him and his family. After that, we'll stay at a hotel until we can find a house or an apartment to rent. School starts next month, so I don't want to wait too long," I replied.

"Are we gonna join the Virginia pack under new names? Or just try to avoid all other werewolves?"

"We're going to have to try joining the pack. Damien's aunt will get suspicious if she has to house rouge wolves. We can keep our first names so things won't get confusing, but we'll need to change our last names. We should probably try to stay away from other werewolves as much as possible, because if someone recognizes Rena and me, they'll turn us in."

Zander just nodded, thinking about what I had said. I decided to ask him a question. "Zander, why did you and Zane come and beat up those guys for us? It's not that I'm not grateful that you did, but we could have handled it ourselves."

"Well we had to defend our girls," he answered with a shy smile.

"Your girls?" I asked with a smirk.

He nodded. "Rena is Zane's girlfriend, and I was going to ask you anyway...," he hesitated for a moment and then said, "Serenity, will you be my girl?" He looked nervous as he asked, but I was ecstatic. I decided to tease him a little bit.

"Hmm," I said as I walked closer to him and stood on my tip toes. "I don't know." I gently put my hand that he wasn't holding, on the side of his neck and leaned in. I hesitated for a moment, looking into his eyes before closing mine. I then softly pressed my lips to his and kissed him. After a few moments, I pulled back and looked into his eyes again, smiling. "Does that answer your question?" I asked him. He nodded and then smiled, leaning in to kiss me again.

After a moment, we heard whistling from down the beach behind us. We pulled apart and looked at Rena, Zane, Damien, and Mike. Of course they had to ruin an amazing moment by being immature. I just shook my head. Still holding Zander's hand, I pulled him back down the beach so we could beat up our friends.

-X-

Later That Night

Mike and Damien had walked to the beach from Damien's house, so they rode with Zander and I to get some food for dinner. We decided on Mexican food, and as we ate, Damien and Mike told us about the high school we would be attending. I could already tell that there would definitely be some teachers that we would and wouldn't like. Zander, Mike, and I were going to be juniors and Damien, Rena, and Zane would be seniors.

After we finished eating, we dropped Mike off at his house and then drove to Damien's. He had already asked, so his aunt didn't have a problem with us staying there.

When we arrived, Tasha gave us a tour of her home. Their house was pretty big, and they had two extra guest rooms. Rena and I shared a room, while Zane and Zander shared the other room. The living room and kitchen were huge, and there was a dining room, study, and three other bedrooms. Each bedroom, including the guest rooms, had its own full bathroom. There was half bathroom on the first floor between the living room and kitchen.

The bedroom Rena and I shared was amazing. It had a king sized bed with bright orange and lime green striped sheets, and a purple comforter. There were black night stands on each side of the bed, with each its own lamp. There was a black desk with an orange chair against one wall, and against another wall, there was a shelf filled with books, DVDs, CD's, and video games. Directly across from the bed was a 32" LCD flat screen TV with a DVD player and a game system. On the other wall, there was an amazing stereo system mounted. An orange painted dresser with a mirror on top sat next the media shelf. There was also a huge closet next to the bathroom. In the bathroom, there was a walk-in shower and a huge jacuzzi tub. A stainless steel sink sat nestled in a black marble counter top, with a mirrored medicine cabinet hanging above. A cabinet across from the sink held purple, orange, and green towels.

Damien's family was definitely very wealthy like mine. Tasha Kaynes, Damien's Aunt, was very high up in the pack. She was a friend of the alpha female. It was a risk, staying with her considering all of the alphas in the country probably knew that we were missing by now. Before coming to stay with Damien, Tasha didn't know us.

All he had told her was that he wanted some friends to stay with them for a little while. He also told her that our parents died so we had gotten emancipated but we didn't have any where else to go yet. Tasha was going to get the paper work so we could join the Virginia pack. She was also going to help us find an apartment or house to rent. When I told her that we could stay in a hotel, she told me no, that we were to stay with them until we found somewhere else to live.

Tasha was a very motherly person; I couldn't believe that she didn't have kids of her own. Danni wasn't even staying at the house. She wanted to go to an all girl's boarding school. I wondered why Tasha didn't know who we were. Damien is a talker and I was sure that he would have told her. When I talked to Damien about it, he said that he didn't really tell her anything personal. I kind of got the impression that he resented her for being the only one who lived through the car crash that killed his parents.

The next morning when Rena and Zane were trying to sneak out to smoke, Tasha caught them. She actually confiscated their pot, and told them that if she found them with it again, she would just take that too. When Rena told me about it, she was in between mad and disappointed because that was all she had left until she could find someone to buy from. Zander told me that Zane was really disappointed too. For the rest of the day, we just hung around Damien's house with him and Mike.

CHAPTER NINE

House for Rent

Our fake IDs were amazing. They looked exactly like our old ones, except with different last names, birthdays, and states. We also had new birth certificates and passports. My name was changed from Serenity Landon to Serenity Starr. Rena Landon became Rena Riddell. Zander Noonan was now Zander Mead and Zane Noonan was now Zane Mead.

Now that we had the new documents, we hid our old ones somewhere safe in case we ever needed them again. Zander and I also signed the title to our truck with our new names. We went and bought new license plates for all of our vehicles so we couldn't be traced by the California and Nevada plates.

We also went out looking for jobs. We all filled out a few applications and a lot of the jobs looked pretty promising. I didn't tell any one else, but I found a house for rent that was perfect. I took down the number so that I could call later. I wanted to check it out before I told everyone.

After we finished our errands, we picked up Damien and Mike and went to see a movie. When we got back to Damien's house,

Tasha had made dinner for us. She was such an amazing cook. I loved cooking and I really wanted to get some of her recipes.

After dinner, Zane, Rena, and Zander hung out in the living room playing video games while Damien drove Mike home. I was in the kitchen with Tasha helping clean up. I decided to tell her about the house I found.

"Tasha, I was wondering if you would come with me to check out a house I saw for rent. I want to surprise everyone else, so I can't tell them yet. I thought that you would most likely know more about getting a house than I do."

"Of course, I'll go with you. Have you called about it yet?" She asked.

"Not yet," I answered. "I was going to call after I was finished helping you."

"Well," she replied. "I have a day off tomorrow so when you call, find out if we can look at it then. If we can, I will have Mike and Damien keep Rena, Zane, and Zander busy while we check it out."

When we finished, I stepped outside and called the number using the prepaid cell phone I bought in Nevada. Someone answered on the third ring.

"Hello?" A woman's voice answered.

"Hi, my name is Serenity and I am calling about a house for rent."

"Yes, are you interested in renting it?"

"Yes, ma'am, I was wondering if I could stop by and look at the house tomorrow."

"That's fine, how about around one o'clock?"

"That will work just fine."

"Okay, I look forward to meeting you tomorrow."

"Thank you," I replied, and hung up.

I walked back into the house to tell Tasha. She said that it was fine and that she would talk to Damien about keeping the others away while we were gone. After we finished talking, we both went into the living room and joined everyone else playing video games until around eleven o'clock. We all went to bed after that because Damien was going to take Zane, Zander, and Rena on a shopping trip while I stayed home to hang out with Tasha.

-X-

The Next Day

After Zander, Zane, Rena, Damien, and Mike left to go shopping at around noon, Tasha and I headed out to see the house. The owner was there leaning on the hood of her car, waiting for us when we arrived. We got out of my truck and walked over to her. I held out my hand to greet her.

"Hello, I'm Serenity Starr, and this is my friend Tasha Kaynes." She took my hand.

"Nice to meet you, my name is Shauna Moore." Shauna was a pretty woman. She looked to be in her mid-thirties, with dark skin and curly dark brown hair. "You were interested in renting the house?" She asked me.

"Yes. I wanted to see the inside and get some information about it." She put her hand in her pocket and pulled out a key.

"Not to be rude, but you seem a little to young to be renting a house. May I ask your age?"

"Well, I'm only sixteen, but the others who would be living here with me are seventeen, eighteen, and nineteen," I told her.

"To tell you the truth, I don't know about renting a house to a bunch of teenagers."

"I completely understand," I replied, "but I promise that we are all really responsible."

Tasha spoke up then. "I'm here to co-sign for her if that makes you feel better. I'm definitely not a teenager," She laughed.

"Okay then. I have to make a phone call, so here is the key. I will meet you inside in a few minutes." She handed it to me and walked away from us.

I looked at the house. It was so beautiful and it was facing the beach. The front yard was covered in sand, with a hammock hanging between two palm trees. The house was built from red bricks and brown tiles made up the roof. Tasha and I went to the front door. I unlocked it and we stepped into a gorgeous living room that was already furnished with an ivory couch and love seat with peach colored throw pillows. The floor was a light colored wood. There was an ivory and peach rug under a small coffee table that matched the floor. The curtains matched the rug. In front of the table was a small wooden stand for a television and entertainment systems.

After I was finished admiring the living room, I moved on to the dining room. It was also completely furnished. The walls were a pale yellow color and there was a large table with six chairs that was made of two different kinds of wood. Under it was a shaggy brown and black rug. On one wall, there were floor to ceiling windows and in between was a china cabinet. On the adjacent wall was a rectangular cabinet that matched the table and chairs.

The kitchen had amazing golden marble counter tops and black cabinets. Above one counter, windows extended across the entire wall. The appliances and sink were made of stainless steel.

There was a half bathroom next to the living room. It had green walls and a brown and white tiled floor. The counter top was brown marble, and it held a white ceramic sink. Above it was a huge mirror that extended almost to the ceiling.

There were four bedrooms and each of them had their own en-suite bathrooms. As I looked at the bedrooms and bathrooms, I was already planning how I would decorate them. I decided that

I wanted the house and would furnish and decorate the bedrooms according to everyone's personalities. I wanted it to be a surprise.

Shauna found Tasha and me in the kitchen discussing possible bedroom plans.

"So how do you like the house?" she asked.

"I love it!" I answered. "I definitely want to rent it. If you decide to sell it, let me know."

She laughed, "I'll make sure that you are the first person I tell. Did you see the basement and the back yard yet?"

"No, we haven't," I answered. "I didn't even know that there was a basement."

Shauna led us through the hallway outside of the kitchen and down a small flight of stairs. When we reached the bottom, I froze. I may have even caught some flies by the way that my mouth was hanging open. Tasha poked me to get my attention so we could continue.

It was the most amazing basement I had ever seen in my life. It had white carpet and there was a black leather sofa and two red leather recliners. There was a massive television inside a wooden entertainment center that was built into the wall. Right beside it was a stone fire place with a high, wooden mantle. A dark curtain separated the room in half. In the other half of the room, there was a pool table.

Shauna and Tasha had to practically drag me back up the stairs. We went out the sliding back doors and I automatically froze again. In the back yard, there was a pool with an attached hot tub surrounded by rock work. There was an elaborate waterfall, and behind it was a hidden water slide. It was the most beautiful back yard I had ever seen.

I turned to look at Shauna. "How much is the rent?" I asked her, "because I definitely have to have this house."

Chapter Ten

A New Home

I spent the next couple weeks avoiding Zane, Zander, and Rena because I wanted to surprise them. Damien, Mike, and Tasha were helping me get the house ready. We fixed it so that my room was right across the hall from Zander's and Rena's was across from Zane's.

I was the only one who hadn't gotten a job yet, so I used the money I had saved up so that I could pay a few months rent in advance. I also had used my money to decorate and furnish the house. I had convinced Shauna to let me paint. I bought a lot of cooking utensils and fully stocked the fridge and cabinets with food, plates, cups, bowls, etc.

After about three weeks, we were finished with the house. We all got back to Tasha's house right before Zane, Zander, and Rena arrived. I had made a copy of the house key for all three of them and I kept the original. When I handed them all a key, they were confused. I told them that I had found a house and that I had already paid rent and fully furnished it. They were all in shock. They knew that I was looking for a house, but they had no idea that I had already found one and was working on it.

"Where did you find the time to do all of that?" Rena asked.

"Well, I had to have something to do while you all worked. Tasha, Damien, and Mike helped me out a lot." They were all staring at me. "Stop gawking at me and let's go see the house!" Tasha, Damien, Mike, and Zander rode in my truck with me and Rena and Zane took her Porsche, following me to our new home.

Once we arrived we all got out of our cars and stood in front of the house. Rena, Zane, and Zander were the only ones who hadn't seen it yet, so they were really excited. They loved the front of the house and the yard. I could tell that they all really liked the hammock. We walked to the front door, and when Rena tried to twist the door knob it was locked. She smiled to herself remembering that she had to use her key. While they were looking at the living room, half bathroom, kitchen, and dining room, I just watched them to see how they would react to the house. We moved to the bedrooms. I had signs made with their names on them and I had hung them on their bedroom doors.

First they looked at Zander's room and bathroom. "Whoa, this is amazing, Serenity," Zander said to me.

His entire bedroom was done in black and white, his favorite colors. It had white walls and light colored wood floors. There was a small indention in the left wall, and a flat screen TV mounted there. Under the TV was a glass shelf that held remotes. The center wall had three windows. On the right wall was a queen sized bed with a black frame. On the bed was a white comforter and pillows with black cases. White painted shelving ran across the entire wall on both sides of the bed, housing some of his favorite books. There was a small, round bedside table and in front of it was a square, black and white rug.

"You didn't have to do all this you know. I would have paid for my own stuff."

"But I wanted to," I answered. "It's like a monster sized gift."

Everyone just smiled. We left Zander to check out his room while we moved on to Zane's.

His room was simple but perfect for him. It had gray carpet and black walls. The bed sat in the center of the room. It had a wooden frame and a black headboard. The sheets and pillow cases were black, and the comforter was various shades of blue. A small, wooden bedside table sat on the right side of the bed and held a blue lamp and a remote. Directly across from the bed was a flat screen mounted on the wall. A shaggy blue rug completed the room. I used so much blue because it was his favorite color.

When he saw it, he just looked at it for a few moments. Then he unexpectedly turned around and walked over to me. He pulled me up into a massive bear hug and mumbled a thank you to me. When he put me down, he went to further inspect his room. I grabbed Rena's hand and took her to look at her's.

For Rena's bedroom, I had decided to bring the outside in. The floors were dark wood and the walls were off-white. There was a large floor mattress that took up one side of the room. It was pale green with a matching comforter and pillows. I didn't get a full sized bed with a frame, because I knew that Rena sometimes tossed and turned in her sleep and I didn't want her to roll off. Across from it was a huge TV that took up most of the wall. Under it was a white shelf that extended the length of the wall. On the center wall was a huge painting of plants and trees that covered the entire wall, and above the bed were two matching paintings of a beach. In the floor were several forest green bean bags. I knew she liked hiking and being outside, so I thought that the woodsy theme would be the perfect design.

When she saw her room she squealed, hugged me, and then ran to her bed and flopped on it. "Don't forget to look at the bathroom," I said, and then walked down the hall to my room.

I decided my room should be done in orange, one of my favorite colors. My walls were white and my floor was made of marble. On one wall were two white wardrobes with orange doors. I had shelves put into them so that instead of holding my clothes, they held my books. In between them was a white desk that held my laptop. My closet door had been painted orange, along with the inside of the bedroom door. On the center wall was my queen sized bed. It had a clear headboard and a metal frame that was hidden by the orange bed skirt. Both my comforter and pillow cases, along with the sheets were orange. There were bedside tables on either side of the bed that matched the head board. In the floor in front of the bed was a shaggy white rug.

The only windows were above my bed, and in the window sill were pictures recently taken of Rena, Zane, Zander, Damien, Mike, and I.

My bathroom was my favorite. The floor was made up of huge orange tiles and the walls were white tiles. There were wall stickers in the shape of orange flowers around the bottom of the wall that went around the entire room. There was a clear, walk-in shower and a white marble sink. Above it was a mirror and under it, was a small white cabinet.

I opened my door and walked inside, flopping face down on my bed. My thoughts returned to the woman I had rented the house from, Shauna. Something about her had bothered me. I didn't know exactly what it was; I hadn't paid much attention to her before because I was so excited about getting the house. Before I could get absorbed in my thoughts, someone knocked on my open door. I lifted my head and looked to see Zander standing there, smiling at me. "Hey," I said to him.

"Hey," he said back, looking around my room. "This is a pretty awesome room."

"Yeah, I know, I saved the best for myself," I said, laughing. I sat up and patted a spot on the bed next to me. He walked over and sat down.

"Thank you for all this," he said.

"It was really no problem. I actually enjoyed doing it."

He smiled at me and then leaned over and kissed me. After a few moments, he pulled back a little bit. "Happy birthday," he whispered, looking into my eyes.

"How did you know that it was my birthday?" I groaned.

"Rena told me. I got you something."

"You really didn't have to get me anything," I said.

"Yeah, right, after everything you've done for everyone, you are seriously gonna tell me that I shouldn't have gotten you anything?" I just shrugged.

"Well, trust me, after the day is over, you will think that what I got you is nothing." He pulled a small box wrapped with star paper out of his pocket. He handed it to me. I sighed and unwrapped it, setting the paper aside and opening the box. I gasped. Inside was a gold and white gold moon and star necklace with diamond accents.

"Oh my God. This is the most beautiful necklace I have ever seen." Zander took the box from me and took the necklace out. I turned my back to him and lifted my hair, so he could put the necklace around my neck. I was so excited that I turned to him and practically tackled him. We sat there kissing until we heard someone clear their throat. We broke apart to see Rena and Zane standing in the doorway.

"Are we interrupting something?" Rena asked with an innocent smile.

I rolled my eyes. "Yeah, actually, you are."

"Well, too bad," she answered. "We have to see the rest of the house." I sighed. Rena skipped out the door with Zane trailing behind her. Zander stood up and held his hand out to me. Taking his offering, I stood up. We walked out and followed Rena and Zane to the basement, and when we got there, their jaws dropped. They were silent for a few moments, and I started to get worried, thinking that they didn't like it. Then the silence was broken by Rena, squealing loudly, again. Zander and Zane couldn't stop smiling and walking around, taking everything in.

"If you think this is awesome, Rena, just wait until you see the back yard," I said. She immediately turned and looked at me with a shocked expression that seemed to say, *what could be better than this?* When she looked at me, I saw that she also had a new necklace. It was a beautiful wolf pendant. I barely had time to notice it before she had taken off, running up the basement stairs. We all followed after her. I almost ran into her when I reached the top of the stairs, she was frozen in place right outside the back door.

"Are you gonna let us out or not?" I asked her. She still didn't move. I pushed her aside so Zander, Zane, and I could get out. When Rena finally started to scream, I walked back inside; she was starting to give me a migraine.

I found Tasha, Damien, and Mike leaning on the counter in the kitchen talking. I walked to the fridge and grabbed a soda. "So I guess Rena really likes everything," Tasha commented.

"Yeah," I answered. "Maybe she likes it a little bit too much." I went over to the counter to join them.

"OMG, I love the necklace, Ren," Damien said.

"Thanks, Damey. Zander gave it to me for my birthday."

"Today is your birthday?" He asked. Damien was lying. He knew it was my birthday and he had always been a horrible liar. I saw Mike roll his eyes.

"Yes, today is my birthday, and you knew that. So what are you planning? Because you know I hate surprises."

"I have no idea what you are talking about," he said unconvincingly.

"Sure you don't," I mumbled.

Zander, Zane, and Rena walked in then, joining us in the

kitchen. Zander came up behind me and put his arms around my waist, leaning me back into his chest as he rested his chin on top of my head.

"When do we get to move in?" Rena asked, excited.

"Whenever you want. All you have to do is get your stuff over here. I already have food here and everything," I said, holding up my soda.

We left soon after to go and get our stuff. Rena wanted to move in immediately, as in, in the next few hours. As we drove back to Tasha's house, everyone was quiet except for a few giggles coming from Damien and Mike. It was starting to get a little annoying. When we got there, I parked the truck and got out. Zander walked over to me and took my hand as we walked to the front door. As I walked into the house, I wasn't expecting what was inside.

CHAPTER ELEVEN

Streamers and a Party Dress

There were purple, orange, and lime green streamers hanging with a Happy Birthday banner. Balloons were everywhere. Caterers were setting up tables of food. I looked over at Zander. He seemed to be amused at the look that was on my face. When Rena walked in, I opened my mouth to question her but she cut me off. "Save the yelling for later. Right now, we have to go get dressed before the guests arrive."

"Guests? But I don't even know anyone here," I complained.

"I'll explain in a few minutes, just come on," she replied. I sighed, giving in and following her. Tasha led us upstairs to her massive bedroom. She gave me a robe to change into and once I was finished, she sat me down in the chair in front of her vanity. After Tasha and Rena both put on robes, Tasha began to do my hair while Rena did my make up. I didn't complain anymore because I knew it wouldn't do me any good. After they were finished with me, they let me look in the mirror. I was shocked at how good I looked.

My hair was pulled back into an elegant, yet simple bun on the back of my head. Tasha had pinned a Caribbean blue flower to the side of my bun. My make up was simple; I just had on light blue eye shadow with a little bit of mascara and lip gloss. My bright blue eyes were impossibly brighter, and my face didn't look over done.

After I approved my hair and makeup, it was my sister's turn. Tasha parted her red hair to the side and pulled it into a half pony tail. Her long wavy locks flowed gracefully down her back. I didn't want to put much make up on her already beautiful face, so I just put a little bit of mascara with some lip gloss to give her a natural look. When we finished with her, somehow, she looked even more beautiful.

We finally sat Tasha down into the chair. I twisted her long brown hair into a French bun and left a wavy lock to hang over the side of her face. Rena put some light purple eye shadow on her and some lip gloss that was the exact shade of her lips. She looked absolutely gorgeous. Rena went down the hall to the room we were staying in to get the dresses that she had apparently bought for the occasion.

She returned with three garment bags in one arm and three shoe boxes in the other. She handed both Tasha and I each a bag and a box. I sat the box on Tasha's bed and unzipped the garment bag. I gasped at the dress. It was mid-thigh length and Caribbean blue. I kept on the necklace from Zander; it would complete my outfit well. Rena stepped into the bathroom with her bag and Tasha went into her walk-in closet. I took the robe off and slipped into the dress. I sat down on the bed and opened the shoe box as Rena was coming out of the bathroom. I pulled out the shoes and looked at Rena in shock. They were glittery, silver peep toe pumps and they were amazing, but I couldn't wear them.

"You really expect me to wear these? You know I like keeping my feet on the ground," I exclaimed.

"Don't complain Serenity. You can handle it for one night," she said, smirking at me.

I rolled my eyes and mumbled, "if I make it through the night." I was an incredibly clumsy person. I tripped over invisible objects all the time. Rena just sighed and shook her head as I slipped on the potentially dangerous, yet beautiful shoes. Tasha came out of her closet and walked over to Rena so she could zip up the back of her dress.

Rena's dress was white and ended just below her knees. It had a black ribbon at the waist that tied into a large bow at her side. Her heels were also glittery and silver. She wore a diamond heart necklace.

While mine and Rena's dresses were strapless, Tasha's purple, knee-length dress had sleeves that stopped at her elbows. Her shoes were made of purple straps and they had rainbow colored rhinestones going down the front. She wore purple bangles on her left wrist.

"You both look amazing," I told them.

"Thank you," Tasha replied with a smile. "So do you." Rena just nodded in agreement.

"So who are all of these mystery guests?" I asked.

"They are some of the students that we will be going to school with, and some of Tasha's friends," Rena replied. "I just had Damien, Tasha, and Mike invite whoever they wanted since we don't know anyone. If this party is as amazing as I know it will be, we'll fit in at school in no time."

I rolled my eyes. Rena had always been the sociable one. I didn't care if anyone liked me or not.

"So, even through my hatred of dresses, I like this one. Did you dress the guys too?" I asked, just wanting to change the subject. I wasn't too excited about going downstairs and meeting a bunch of strangers. I had never been a people person.

"Nope," she answered. "I let Damien do that. At least we know that they'll look good. He's seen the dresses, so the colors won't clash. That would have been a disaster."

"Oh, yes, the world would have ended if their ties didn't match our dresses," I said sarcastically, rolling my eyes. Rena growled at me. "You are so scary, Rena," I said as I pretended to shake in fear. We both couldn't help ourselves after that, we had to laugh.

My cell phone started vibrating on the dresser. I walked over to get it. Zander had sent me a text.

R u almost done? Damien is torturing us.

LOL. Yes we r done. Is any1 here yet?

Yes. There r a lot of people downstairs.

K. Meet u @ the top of the stairs.

I flipped my cell phone closed and set it back down on the dresser. "Okay, let's go. Damien is torturing our boyfriends."

Rena laughed and headed out the door. I started to follow, but Tasha grabbed my arm. "Serenity, I didn't want to ruin Rena's good mood but, the Virginia alpha is going to be here. I think he wants to speak to you four." She was clearly concerned about what would happen during that conversation.

"Okay," I nodded. "Do you know if he is going to let us join the pack?"

"I think he will. He hasn't turned anyone down yet." We then went out the door to follow Rena to the staircase. She was already there talking to the guys.

"Hey, Serenity," Zander said as he walked to my side and took my hand. He gave me an admiring look as he took in my dress. "You look beautiful," he told me and kissed my cheek.

I blushed a little at his compliment.

"Thanks," I mumbled. I looked at what they were wearing. All of the guys were wearing dress shirts and ties to match their outfit. Zander was wearing a blue tie the exact shade of my dress. Zane's tie was black, and both Damien and Mike's ties were hot pink. "You four look pretty nice yourself."

Tasha walked down the stairs first, and met a man at the bottom.

It was probably her boyfriend. Damien and Mike walked down next, holding hands. After them were Rena and Zane. Then it was our turn. Zander squeezed my hand lightly. He could tell that I was nervous. We descended the stairs hand in hand.

There were a lot of people in Tasha's huge front room. All the furniture was pushed against the wall and the dining room table had been moved to make more room. My CD's were being played by a DJ that was set up in a corner. We hadn't eaten all day, so Zander and I made our way over to the tables where the food was.

After we ate a little, one of my favorite slow songs came on. Zander asked me to dance. After I accepted the invitation, he walked me to the middle of the room and pulled me close to him, taking one of my hands in his and putting his other on my waist. I rested my head on his chest as we danced. When another slow song came on, I looked up at him. He leaned down and kissed me.

"I love you," he murmured against my lips.

I pulled back just a little bit and looked into his eyes. They were full of love and admiration. That was the very first time that he told me that he loved me. I smiled.

"I love you, too," I replied sincerely and kissed him again.

For the next hour or so, we just talked and mingled and danced. He never left my side. We found Rena and Zane and were talking to them when a man came up behind me and tapped me on the shoulder. I froze. I could smell him. He was a werewolf. I spun around to face him.

"I need to talk to you four," he said and then motioned for us to step outside.

CHAPTER TWELVE

Broken Trust and Stupidity

The werewolf led us outside and across the yard. He stopped under a tree and turned to look at us. He was taller than Zane. His dark brown hair and brown eyes paired with his sharp features made him look a little intimidating.

"You're Serenity, correct?" he asked me.

"Uh, who wants to know?" I asked, hesitantly.

"Greg Olden, the Virginia pack alpha wants to know," he said.

Of course. I felt stupid. Tanya told me he was going to be here. "Then, yes, I'm Serenity."

"And this is Rena, Zane, and Zander, right?" he asked, pointing to them. I nodded in confirmation.

He gave me a concerned, yet serious look. "You know, your father is looking for you."

I froze in shock. At first, I didn't think that I heard him correctly, but then I looked at Rena and my friends. Their shocked expressions mirrored mine. I looked back at the alpha in front of me.

"Um," I mumbled. "Our father is dead."

"I'm not blind. Isn't this you and your sister?" He held up a flier with a picture of Rena and me with our names on it. "Serenity and Rena Landon. You can change your names, but not your faces."

"How did you find out about us?" I asked, still in shock. "We didn't turn in the papers about joining the pack yet."

"You know Shauna Moore, right? I think you are renting a house from her?" I nodded.

"Well, I guess you didn't notice, but she is a made-werewolf and my assistant." Most werewolves are born, but some people can make werewolves. I don't know how to do it, but some can. Their smell is less distinct than born werewolves. That's probably why I didn't notice before.

"So she was calling you when she said that she needed to make a call," I guessed. He nodded. "Well I'm not going back to California. I'll die before I go back and marry the Nevada brothers." He nodded again.

"I never thought that you would. If I was put in your situation when I was younger, I would have done the same thing." I sighed in relief. "But Zander and Zane's situation is a little more serious," he said, turning towards them. "The Nevada pack wants you dead."

"The Nevada pack?" I asked. "Why? They are from the Washington pack."

"I don't know where you got your information, but they are from the Nevada pack, and they are wanted dead."

I turned to Zander. "You told me that you were from Washington."

"I know, I'm sorry," he said to me quickly, looking regretful. "I had to tell you that so you would trust us and so you wouldn't think that we would turn you in."

"And yet you expect me to trust you now? You've had plenty of time to tell me the truth. Why haven't you?"

"I promise I was going to tell you. I was just waiting for the right time."

"Out of all the times we were alone and talking, you could have said something. You know, when you lie to gain trust, you just lose trust." I turned back to Greg. "Rena will give you my cell number," I said, and then walked away.

I walked back into Tasha's house and went upstairs. I knocked on her door. When no one replied I opened the door and walked in. I went over to her dresser and grabbed my cell phone, and walked back out, shutting her door. I then walked to the room that Rena and I shared. I went in and grabbed my bags out of the closet and put all of my belongings into them except for a pair of ripped, skin-tight jeans, my black T-shirt that says "Bite Me", and my plain black converse sneakers. I changed out of my dress into the clothes and put my dress back into the garment bag and the heels into the box. I also grabbed my wallet with a chain that hooks onto my jeans and crammed it in my pocket, attaching it to my belt loop. I left all of the bags on the bed; I knew Rena would grab them. I walked back downstairs and out the front door.

I got my motorcycle and helmet out of the garage and pushed it into the drive way. I looked over to the tree across the yard. They were all still there talking. Before I put on my helmet, I let my hair down. I started my bike and looked back to the tree. They were all staring at me. I tried my best not to show any emotion, though I knew they couldn't see my face. I turned away and drove off.

-X-

Rena

We had just finished explaining Zane and Zander's accusations and our history with Nevada when I heard Serenity's motorcycle start up. All of our heads turned to the noise. Serenity looked over to us. I couldn't see her expression because of the helmet, but I recognized her shaky posture. My sister was trying not to cry. The revelation sent a burst of fury through me. Of course I knew they were from Nevada. Zane had told me a while back. I figured that Zander had told her by now. I would definitely be having a talk with him soon, but for now, I had to figure things out with Mr. Olden.

I looked back at the Virginia Alpha as Serenity rode away. "So can we join the pack?" I asked him in a semi-pleading voice. He looked a bit hesitant. "I promise, Mr. Olden. You never even saw us. No one knows who we are; you won't get into any trouble. Please, Mr. Olden. Please."

Greg Olden sighed. "Fine. But this meeting never happened. You four are just more application forms entered into the system. Though if I hear anything from either California or Nevada concerning you, I'll let you know." With a last small smile, he returned to the house.

As soon as he was inside, I spun around to face Zander. I could tell he was waiting for it. I slapped him. His head whipped to the side from all of the force I put into it. When he turned back to me, I could see that he felt remorse.

"What the hell, Zander?" I screamed at him. "Why didn't you tell her? I warned you not to hurt her. She's already been through too much."

He looked pleadingly at me. "I know, Rena! I wanted to tell her, I just wanted to wait for the right time. I know that's a pathetic excuse, but I love her. I didn't want this to happen. I feel so bad that I hurt her and just threw more stress on her. And on her birthday, too!"

He ran his hands through his hair and groaned. I kept my glare in place. I noticed Zane looking a bit frightened, cowering in the shadows.

"I'm sorry, Rena. I really am."

"I know, Zander." My expression softened for a moment before turning fierce again. I couldn't help it. My hand swung and hit him in the face again. "That was for ruining the perfect party I planned out." I huffed before turning back to the house.

As soon as I walked in, I went to the DJ and told him to turn off the music. I grabbed his microphone. "Okay everyone. The birthday girl is pissed. Party's over, go home!" There was a chorus of groans before everyone started to file out. As soon as the door shut Tasha's housekeepers set to work, restoring the house to normal.

After explaining everything to Damien and Mike and making up a story for Tasha, I went upstairs to gather our things. I was surprised to see Serenity's bags already packed and on the bed. I knew Serenity had to be pissed. Zander was in for hell when she got home.

-X-

Serenity

I rode around for a while, not knowing where to go. I finally decided on going to a club that I had seen earlier, hoping I could get someone to buy me a drink. I just wanted to get my mind off of Zander before I would start crying. I knew my reaction was immature, but I couldn't help it.

It was about fifteen minutes before I could find it again. I parked my bike and took off my helmet. I fixed my hair in the little rear view mirror and then walked into the club. I looked around for a moment. One of my favorite songs came on, so I moved to the dance floor and started dancing. After about two songs, I saw two really hot guys dancing alone. I watched for a little while as I was dancing to see if there was any one with them. After a few minutes of seeing them alone, I moved closer to them and kept dancing where I knew they would see me. After the song was over, I walked away towards an empty table, knowing that one of them would follow me. I sat down and waited for a moment. When I heard a chair move beside me, I looked up and smiled. The guy that followed me sat down. He had dark hair and brown eyes. He seemed to be in his mid-twenties and was absolutely gorgeous.

"Hello, I'm Alex."

"Hey. Nice to meet you, Alex. I'm Serenity."

"That's a beautiful name. Can I buy you a drink?" he asked.

"Thank you, that would be great," I answered.

"I'll be right back," he said, and walked towards the bar. I unconsciously played with my necklace while I waited. A couple minutes later, he came back with two blue colored drinks. I had no idea what they were, so I sipped mine carefully. It was really good, but I could tell that it contained a lot of alcohol.

"Thanks," I said with a smile.

"No problem. That's a nice necklace," he commented. I then realized that I was playing with it.

"Yeah, a friend of mine gave it to me for my birthday today. The day didn't turn out so well, though," I replied, dropping the necklace.

"I'm sorry your day didn't go well. But maybe it will get better... Happy Birthday." He smiled at me. I returned the smile. We talked for a little while about random things. Then he asked me if I would dance with him. I said yes, and he led me out to the dance floor. As we danced, I noticed I was stumbling a little. I guess that drink contained more alcohol than I had thought.

After dancing to a couple songs, Alex unexpectedly kissed me. I pushed him away. "Don't do that," I snapped. He rolled his eyes and had a look on his face that seemed to say, 'Yeah, like you could stop me.' When he tried again I stepped back, which made him angry. He grabbed my left wrist and pulled me to him. I was definitely not in a good enough mood to just pull away again, so instead, I punched him in the nose, hard. He staggered back. "I said, don't do that," I told him and walked away toward the bar.

"Give me one of those blue thingies please." The bar tender could tell the mood I was in, and I was almost positive that he saw me punch Alex, so he didn't ask me for my ID. I handed him the money. After I was finished with my drink, I left the club. I knew that I probably shouldn't ride my motorcycle considering I was pretty drunk, but I definitely wasn't going to call Rena, Zander, or Zane for a ride. So, I was out of options. I put on my helmet, climbed on my bike, and rode off.

I handled the bike pretty well for someone who had been drinking. I rode to our new house. When I parked my bike and got off, of course, being me, I stumbled and fell. I cursed as I hit the ground. I got up and took off my helmet, putting it with the bike. Both the truck and Rena's Porsche were here. I walked to the front door, unlocked it, and stumbled my way into the house. There was a light on in the kitchen, so I quietly shut the door and locked it. I tried to tip-toe to my room, but of course I tripped and fell into a little table in the hallway. I steadied myself, hoping no one heard me, but of course they did, with their perfect werewolf hearing. Zander came out of the kitchen, wearing black pajama pants and a T-shirt. As we stood there looking at each other, I knew he could smell the alcohol on me.

"Were you drinking, Serenity?"

"Duh," I answered, rolling my eyes. I turned and tried to go to my room. Zander grabbed my arm. I wasn't thinking clearly, I just knew that I was angry, so I swung at him, trying to hit him. I think he knew what I was going to do, because he caught my fist before it could make contact with his face. When he looked down at it, his eyes widened a little bit. When I looked, I saw that my knuckles were bleeding and swollen. I didn't know that I had hit Alex hard enough to fracture my knuckles. But I was satisfied to know that he was probably hurting more than I was.

Zander still had a hold on my arm, so he led me into the kitchen and made me sit down on one of the stools in front of the island. He got a first aid kit from on top of the refrigerator and sat down on the stool beside me. He started fixing up my hand. "So I guess I'm not the only one you were throwing punches at tonight, huh?" he asked.

I rolled my eyes again. "No... Some idiot at the club I was at tried to kiss me. Of course I hit him." Zander chuckled. We sat in silence for a moment. "You know, this is the second time that you have played doctor for me. You are really good at it. I don't even have any scars from the first time." I smiled at him. "Thank you."

"You're welcome," he replied as he finished bandaging my hand.

"I'm really sorry for lying to you, but I had my reasons. I also think it's time for you to know why my family and I were convicted." The seriousness of his tone sobered me up enough to comprehend what he was saying.

"When we were in Nevada, Zane and I went to school with Trevor and Matt Krate. One day in the restroom, we overheard them talking about killing their father. They had a completely thought out plan. After their father was dead, they were going to marry the daughters of the California alpha so that they could take it over when they reached twenty-one. They said something about loosing a war to California years ago, and that they were going to gain the territory at any cost. After we heard all of that, we couldn't just confront them, so we told our parents, who went to the Nevada alpha. Of course he didn't believe us, so we were charged with treason. We were put in jail until the alpha died of a 'heart attack'," Zander made air quotes with his fingers as he emphasized the last two words.

"Once he was dead, Matt and Trevor had our sentence maximized to the death penalty. Zander and I were able to escape, and it was pure coincidence and luck that we found you two in the woods. I promise I was going to tell you, but it slipped my mind every time we were alone and I had the chance to say something. I know I have lost your trust, but I will do everything I can to get it back."

I was silent for a few moments, just looking at him in shock.

"I'm sorry for the way I reacted earlier," I told him truthfully. "I understand why you had to lie to me. And I do still trust you."

"You had every right to be mad at me. And you were right, there were plenty of times I could have told you."

"That may be true, but we all make mistakes," I said as I stood up. He steadied me when I stumbled. "Like getting drunk," I mumbled. He just laughed. Zander helped me to my room. As he turned away, I stopped him. "Will you stay in here with me tonight?" I asked him. He nodded and went to sit on my bed while I got a pair of basketball shorts and a tank top out of one of my bags, which were lying by my closet. I went into the bathroom and successfully changed without falling on my face. I went back into my room and turned off the light. Zander and I got under my cover and I snuggled into his arms.

"I love you, Serenity."

"I love you too, Zander," I replied, and yawned. I quickly drifted off to sleep, feeling safe and content in the arms of the best guy in the world.

Chapter Thirteen

First Day Friends

The rest of the week was uneventful. We all got settled into our new house. Damien and Mike were almost always there. All of the guys were enjoying the basement while we enjoyed the pool and hot tub. I finally found a job to take up some of my free time. We all tried to work around the same time so we would be able to spend our time off hanging out together.

The day before school started, Damien made us all take a shopping trip to the mall. I got some amazing new clothes for school. Damien made us all model some of our clothes so he could give his seal of approval. After we finished, we went out for lunch. We all kept telling jokes and making each other laugh. The manager had to come to our table and tell us to quiet down or we would have to leave. That just made us laugh even harder. For some reason, we were incredibly hyper. When we were finished with lunch, Damien and Mike went home. Zane, Zander, Rena, and I got back to our house, put our clothes away, and changed into our pajamas. Then we headed to the basement with a couple movies and some popcorn.

After a huge popcorn war, I fell asleep sometime during the

second movie. I vaguely remember Zander carrying me to my room. The next thing I knew, my alarm clock was going off. I groaned and lifted my head to look at it. It was six o'clock in the morning. I hit the snooze button and went back to sleep. It went off again ten minutes later. I was irritated and really didn't want to get up, so I ripped the plug out of the wall and threw the clock across the room. It hit the wall with a bang. I fell asleep again instantly. A little while later, Zander was in my room gently shaking me awake. I groaned.

"Honey, you have to get up for school." I sighed and sat up. Since I threw my clock, I had to grab my cell phone from the bedside table to check the time. I gasped and shot out of bed when I saw that it was almost seven. I ran into my bathroom so I could take a shower and heard Zander laugh. After I got out, I dried my hair and straightened it out. I applied some black eyeliner and a little bit of dark purple eye shadow. I put on a long sleeved, black and dark gray striped shirt that had a hood, and threw on a pair of artfully destroyed skinny jeans and my new black on black extra high converse high tops.

I grabbed my wallet and my cell phone, putting them in my pockets as I hurried out of my room with my book bag filled with school supplies. I found Zander, Zane, and Rena all waiting for me in the living room. Rena was wearing a plain black long sleeved shirt with light colored jeans and ankle high black boots. Her long red hair was pulled into a wavy pony tail with her newly cut bangs hanging over one side of her face. Zander had on a pair of black jeans and a t-shirt with a black jacket. Zane was the only one wearing any color other than black. He was wearing a red t-shirt. With it, he wore faded blue jeans. Both guys wore black converse low tops, and they looked pretty hot.

We hurried out the door and into our separate vehicles, Zander and I in the truck and Rena and Zane in the Porsche. Before heading to the school, I went through the drive through at *Starbucks*. We ordered a couple of cheese croissants and two java chip frappuccinos.

We ate as I drove. I knew the way to the school, since Damien had brought me here the other day so I could make sure that we all got registered. I had gotten all of our class schedules. Zander only had three out of seven classes with me. I had one with Rena and two with Zane.

I pulled into the parking lot, finding a fairly close parking spot next to Rena's car. Zander and I finished eating and then got out of the truck. As we walked hand in hand into the building, quite a few people were staring at us. I wondered if Zane and my sister had gotten this much attention. We found our lockers which were all side by side, and Rena and Zane were already there, waiting for us. I pulled my information sheet out of my book bag and looked for my locker combination. I opened the locker to see that my text books were already in it, with my name printed neatly inside each one. I put my empty notebooks into the locker and arranged it by class. Then I shoved my book bag in and checked my schedule again.

Serenity Starr- Grade 11

English 11/Room 123- Mr. Kroh
Spanish 3/Room 221- Sra. Alverz
American Government/Room 224- Mr. Chung
Physical Education/Gymnasium- Mr. Pleasant
Astronomy/Room 310- Mrs. Monaco
Lunch
Geometry/Room 210- Mr. Pointdatwai
Cooking/Room 132- Mrs. Brennan

Principal- Mr. Cooke\Assistant Principal- Mr. Frasure

I pulled out the books for my first two classes and grabbed two notebooks. I shut my locker and folded my schedule and the information sheet to put them in the back pocket that wasn't housing my wallet. I looked at Zander who was just shutting his locker.

"Ready?" he asked me. I nodded and we walked to our first class calling out a quick "See you later," to Rena and Zane. Our first class was English 11. We introduced ourselves to the teacher, Mr. Kroh, and he told us to sit wherever we wanted. There were a few empty seats in the back, so we went and sat down in two of them. I was surprised when Mike walked into the classroom. I hadn't checked my schedule with his. He sat in the seat on the other side of Zander. He waved at us, and then looked around the room, probably to see if there were any of his friends in this class.

A girl with light brown curly hair sat down beside me. She was a beautiful girl who looked to be around sixteen. Along with her textbooks and notebooks, she had two huge novels. She pulled a cute pair of glasses out of her purse and put them on. She opened one of the novels and read until the bell signaling the start of class rang. She put the book away and took off the glasses and sat them on her desk.

Mr. Kroh came to the front of the room. "Since today is our first day of school, you can spend the class period talking to your neighbors and getting to know each other. But keep your voices down." He went back to his desk and propped his feet up, opening an Edgar Allan Poe novel.

The girl beside me was about to open her book again when I decided to talk to her. "Hello," I said to her. She looked at me like she was shocked that someone was talking to her. "I'm Serenity."

"Uh, I'm Courtney," she mumbled. Her voice was kind of preppy sounding, but with a nervousness to it that showed that she wasn't used to talking to people much.

"Nice to meet you, Courtney. This is my boyfriend Zander, and our friend, Mike," I said, pointing to them. They both smiled and waved. "We are new here and I was wondering if you could show us around?"

She smiled at me and nodded. "Do you want to sit with me and my friends at lunch?" She asked.

"Sure, do you mind if a couple of my friends join us?"

"No problem, it's not like our table is full or anything." She giggled. I smiled at her. We talked until the bell rang. I told her my locker number, and she said that she would meet us there before lunch.

I had Spanish 3 with Damien and Rena next. When I arrived in class, I invited them to sit with Courtney and I at lunch. They accepted. After the bell rang and all the students were in their seats, a very small, yet intimidating Hispanic woman walked into the class room.

"*¡Hola! ¿Cómo estas?*" She greeted.

I immediately answered. "*Muy bien. ¿Y tú?*"

She smiled. "*Muy bien. Gracias.*"

"*No hay de que.*"

"Well," she said with a heavy accent. "At least someone practiced their Spanish over break." She went to her desk and sat down. "You can talk this period, but only if you speak in Spanish. If I hear any English being spoken, I will give you an assignment, and possibly your first detention of the year." Wow, she definitely wasn't a teacher that I was going to like. As she was taking roll, Rena took her chance to tell her off.

"Rina Riddell?" As soon as I heard her pronunciation of Rena's name, I knew Rena was going to be mad. She hated when someone pronounced her name wrong.

"My name isn't Rina," she snapped. "It's Rena. Ree-na." The death glare she gave Sra. Alverz was enough for her to apologize and move on quickly. I couldn't help the small laugh I let out.

All of my morning classes went by pretty quickly. Before I knew it, I was meeting Courtney at my locker for lunch. When Zander and I got there, she was already waiting for me. I gave her a quick hello, and then put my books into my locker. We waited for Rena, Zane, Damien, and Mike. They all soon arrived and we walked to the lunch room together. We went through the line, grabbing a tray and some random food, paying for it at the end. After I put my wallet back into my back pocket, I followed Courtney to a table. She sat down by the first Hispanic guy I had ever seen with an afro. He dressed in black clothes that made him look like a ninja. When I saw his face, I immediately knew that he was high. I giggled a little. He looked worse off than Zane and Rena.

"This is Torak," Courtney introduced him. "But we call him Shorty, like in Scary Movie." She laughed.

"Hey Shorty," I said with a grin. "I'm Serenity."

"Waz up?" He dragged out, causing me to laugh. Everyone introduced themselves. As we ate, Rena and Zane were extremely interested in Shorty. Probably for their pot head purposes.

About half way through lunch, I took a deep breath through my nose. I immediately realized that there were seven werewolves in the room instead of the six I was expecting. As I looked around, I realized who the seventh werewolf was. I was shocked. It was Shorty.

CHAPTER FOURTEEN

Afro Ninjas and Nerds

I stared at him in shock. I couldn't believe that I hadn't noticed his scent before. But with the heavy odor of marijuana, it was hard to smell anything.

"Uh, Serenity, are you okay?" Rena interrupted my daze.

"Yeah, I'm fine," I answered, pulling my cell phone out of my pocket. I turned it to the side and flipped it up, sending Zander a text. When his phone vibrated, he jumped a little and then pulled out his phone. When he saw the text, he almost choked on the bite of food he was swallowing.

Shorty is a werewolf!!!!

What? R u sure?

Yes! I can just barely smell him.

Now that u mention it, I can 2.

I'll talk 2 him l8er.

K.

I put my cell phone back in my pocket. After we finished lunch, I waited for everyone to get ahead. Shorty was walking a little slow, like he knew that I needed to talk to him.

"Um, Shorty, can I talk to you?"

"Yup." He stopped walking but I waited until everyone else was ahead before I started talking.

"So, do you already know what I want to talk to you about?" I asked.

"Yeah, I may be high, but that doesn't mean I'm stupid. You want to talk about me being a werewolf."

"Uh, well, yeah, are you part of the pack?"

"Nope. This afro ninja runs alone."

I smirked. "Afro ninja?"

"Uh huh, can't you tell?"

"A little, but that's not important. Rena and I are runaways from California. Zander and Zane are wanted dead. We need to know that if anyone comes asking, you won't turn us in."

He laughed a little. "Why would I turn in my new friends? It will be nice to have more than one wolf in the school. I won't have to run around for our once a year, full moon phase alone."

Most people think that werewolves can't help but change every full moon. But really, only once a year on a full moon, all werewolves have to phase. It's a random thing, it happens at a different full moon every year. We can feel it about a week before when the change is going to happen, so were always prepared.

I laughed, relieved. "Thank you, Shorty!" I hugged him. He chuckled and hugged me back. As we were walking to our lockers, which happened to be right across the hall from each other, he decided to tease me.

"You know, you have a lot of stress. Maybe you should try smoking." He grinned.

"Yeah, I'd rather not," I replied, smiling back. We exchanged numbers, and then went to our lockers. Zander was waiting for me at mine.

"So, how did it go?" he asked.

"It went fine. He's not part of the pack, he's a lone wolf," I smiled. "He's not going to turn us in."

"That's good." I opened my locker and got out my geometry and cooking textbooks. "So what are we doing after school?" I grabbed a couple note books and a pencil, and then shut my locker.

"Rena wants to invite Damien and Mike over to the house later to hang out. I'm going to invite Courtney and Shorty, too." Zander nodded. I gave him a hug and then hurried to geometry. When I entered the class room, I saw Zane. I went and sat by him.

"Hey Zane."

"Hey Ren, did you talk to Damien and Mike yet?"

"No, I forgot about it until just a few minutes ago." He nodded. The bell rang and the teacher stood up at his desk. After he called roll, he introduced himself.

"Hello class, we have new students this year." He pointed to Zane and me and said our names. "My name is Mr. Pointdatwai," he told us. His name caused the whole class to giggle. His name sounded kind of like *point that way*.

Class went by pretty slow. When it was over, I had cooking class with Zane, too. Finally, the first day of school was over. I put my books in my locker in a hurry, and went to find Courtney.

When I found her, she was just closing her locker.

"Hey Courtney, do you want to come over to my house and hang out? I'm gonna invite Damien, Mike, and Shorty, too."

"Sure, when?"

"Right now, you can follow me to my house." We started walking to the parking lot.

"Okay, but we will have to talk to Shorty first. He gives me a ride to and from school. Are Rena, Zane, and Zander coming too?"

"Oh, Yeah, I guess I forgot to tell you, but all four of us live together."

"That's cool. Don't your parents care?"

"Well, my mom and dad died. Rena's parents died, too. They were all in a car crash together. Zane and Zander just didn't get along with their parents, so we all got emancipated."

I told her our rehearsed story. We were in the parking lot now and I followed her to where we saw Shorty standing by his car. It was a 2009 black Nissan Maxima.

"Do you want to go hang out at Serenity's house?" Courtney asked him.

"Sure. Do you want me to just follow you?" He asked me.

"Yeah, I'm parked just a few cars down. It's the black Ford F150." He looked at it.

"Nice truck," he commented. "Is it yours?"

"Yes, Zander and I bought it together." He nodded and then got into his car. Courtney got in as I walked to the truck, pulling out my cell phone. I sent a quick text to Damien and Mike.

Can u come 2 my house rite now? Rena wants us 2 hang out. I sent this to both of them. Damien replied first.

Yep. What r we doing?

I have no idea.

Mike answered a few moments later.

I guess. Is Damien gonna be there?

Yeah.

K. I'll be there.

I put my phone into my pocket and got into the truck. Zander was already there. "Shorty and Courtney are following us," I told him.

"Are they in the black Nissan?" He asked.

"Yep," I answered. I started the truck and pulled out of the parking lot. I made sure Shorty was still following us, and then headed towards the house.

CHAPTER FIFTEEN

Truth or Dare

When we got to the house, I pulled into the garage. Rena's car was already there. Zander and I got out of the truck and walked out into the drive way. Shorty was pulling in and once he was parked, he turned off the car and he and Courtney got out. They followed us to the front door and into the house. When everyone was in the living room, I saw that Rena and Zane were sitting on the love seat. I asked my sister to give Shorty and Courtney a tour of the house, because they were looking around in amazement. She got up and the three of them disappeared down the hallway.

As soon as I sat down on the couch, I heard a horn honk outside. "It's probably Damien and Mike," I said out loud. Zander went to let them in. A moment later, the tree of them came into the living room. They sat down to wait for Rena, Shorty, and Courtney to come back. After a few minutes, they were back and could tell that Rena was up to something.

"Let's go into the basement," Rena said. We followed her down stairs and she ordered us to sit in a circle on the floor. "We're playing Truth or Dare." Everyone groaned, "Don't be babies. Zander, you start."

"Wait!" I exclaimed, remembering something. "Today was the first day of school and Zane and Zander didn't run through the hallways in their underwear! I guess we all forgot."

"Well... to tell you the truth," Zander started, "I did forget up until lunch." I gave him an evil look.

"I didn't forget. I just knew that you all would," Zane told us. Rena punched him in the shoulder making him wince. Courtney and Shorty looked really confused, while Damien and Mike just laughed.

"Well, looks like you are going to have to do it tomorrow," I told them. "And as punishment for '*forgetting*'," I said this with air quotes, "You have to run through Señora Alverz's class room too." Zane and Zander gave me the death glare.

"Before we get into a dog fight," Rena said with a smirk, "let's just start the game. You get to start Zander."

He thought for a moment, and then grinned. "Truth or Dare, Zane?"

"Dare."

"I dare you to kiss Damien on the cheek, sorry Damien." We all laughed. Zane looked shocked for a moment, and then shrugged. He turned to Damien, who was sitting beside him, and quickly pecked him on the cheek. Damien giggled and turned red, making everyone laugh even harder.

"Truth or Dare, Mike?" Zane asked.

"Dare."

"You have to stand up and sing a random, girly song." Mike looked really embarrassed as Zane pulled him up. Then he started to sing.

We were all shocked. Mike had a great voice. He sang the song perfectly, not missing any notes. Damien looked at his boyfriend with a proud look on his face. We all clapped, making Mike blush as he went to sit back down.

"Truth or Dare, Courtney?"

"Dare," she replied.

"I dare you to lick the bottom of Damien's foot," Mike grinned. Courtney just looked disgusted, making everyone laugh. Damien removed his left shoe and sock and held his foot out to Courtney with a smirk, knowing she wouldn't do it.

She held her nose and quickly licked his foot, immediately staring to wipe off her tongue with her shirt after she was done. Damien kept saying "Ew, ew, ew," in a girly squeal and tried to clean the spit off of his foot with his sock. Everyone else just laughed. After Damien got his shoe back on, it was Courtney's turn.

"Shorty, Truth or Dare?"

"Dare."

"I dare you to wear one of Rena's outfits for the rest of the day." He just shrugged and stood up. Zane gave him a weird look.

"I just don't get embarrassed easily," Shorty explained and followed Rena up the stairs and to her room.

A few minutes later, they came back down. Everyone in the room, including Shorty and Rena, started laughing hysterically. "Rena, you were supposed to dress him in one of your outfits, not make him look like a hooker," I said to my sister.

"Well he said it had to be black, so I just picked out a few things," she said with a giggle. Shorty was wearing A LOT of lace. His shirt was made of silk and covered in black lace, his short black skirt was layered with silk and lace. He also wore three inch black heels. He looked like he belonged on the street corner, not in my basement.

They sat down and we continued the game, "Serenity, Truth or Dare," Shorty asked.

"Dare," I said, and immediately regretted it when I saw the smile on his face.

"Serenity, you are too much of a goody-goody. You have to get your belly button pierced and get a tattoo."

"Hell no!" I told him.

"Okay," he said with a sigh. "I just thought you were the kind of person who wouldn't turn down a dare." Of course he had to say that, now I had to do it.

"Fine," I said with a sigh. "But we better go and do it now before I change my mind." Shorty yanked me off of the ground and dragged me up the stairs. Everyone else followed us into the garage. We didn't want to take a lot of cars, so Zane and Rena took her car and Zander, Damien, Mike, Shorty, and Courtney took the truck. I rode my motorcycle.

Damien drove the truck and we all followed him since he knew where the best tattoo and piercing shop was. When we got there, I was so freaked out that I couldn't move. So Shorty took the liberty of picking me up like a sack of potatoes and carried me into the building while everyone laughed. He put me down at the front desk. The woman behind the desk gave him a funny look, not because he carried me, but because he was still wearing Rena's clothes. I told the woman what I wanted and she gave me some paper work to fill out. Rena had to sign everything. She was 18, so she was "technically" standing in as my legal guardian.

After we were finished with the papers, I looked through the tattoo books until I found the perfect one. It was huge, but I loved it. It was a series of black and red stars and swirls. They would start in the middle of my lower back and spread out to both sides and go up to the middle of my back. I showed the woman and she told me that the tattoo would take a couple of hours to do. No one wanted to wait around that long, so they went back to the house to finish the game, leaving me the motorcycle. Zander was the only one to stay with me.

When the woman led Zander and I into a room, there was a bald man with a lot of tattoos and piercings sitting in a rolling chair. The woman gave him the picture of what I wanted and he motioned for me to sit down in the chair across from him with my back facing him. I made Zander pull up a chair and hold my hand the entire time. It hurt really badly so I clenched my teeth and buried my head in my arm so I wouldn't scream. After a couple hours, he finished up. He properly wrapped it up and told me how to care for it.

Soon after, he did my belly button. It didn't hurt nearly as bad as the tattoo had. The ring I had put in was silver with three stars hanging down. The top star was the smallest and it had white rhinestones in it. The second star had light blue rhinestones and the last star had dark blue rhinestones and it was the biggest. I bought two other rings to put in later. They were both star themed, too.

When I was finished, Zander led me outside to my bike. I had taught Zander to ride it a couple weeks ago, so he drove us home. When we got there, everyone was gone except for Rena and Zane. Rena promised everyone that I would show them the piercing tomorrow and the tattoo when it was healed. I made a promise to myself; I was going to punch Shorty tomorrow for how much pain I had gone through.

Chapter Sixteen

Prom Night

The next few months went along about the same. Shorty, Courtney, Damien, Mike and the rest of us all hung out together almost every day. After Zane and Zander humiliated themselves by running through the school and into Señora Alverz's classroom in their underwear, they got detention for a week. It was extremely hilarious. The entire school talked about it for a month.

Soon, prom was right around the corner. Of course, Zander and I were going together. Zane asked Rena and Damien and Mike were going together. We were all surprised when Shorty asked Courtney. She accepted and all of us girls, plus Damien, went shopping. We were gone for hours until we found the perfect dresses.

Rena's dress was blood red and form fitting, flaring out a little at mid thigh, and finishing her look with red heels. Courtney's dress was an aqua blue and strapless. Her heels were clear and silver and went perfectly with the dress. My dress was strapless and in various shades of purple. My strappy sliver heels matched the glitter on my dress. Damien got a pink tie to go with his tux, and also bought the other guy's ties to match our dresses.

The day of prom, Tasha forced all of us girls to come to her house to get ready. She and Courtney immediately became friends. We took time to catch up since we hadn't talked for a while. We hung out together and talked while Tasha did our hair and make-up, which took hours. When we put our dresses and shoes on, she made us model them while she took pictures. Rena and I had already started to think of Tasha as another mom.

Our mom was killed two years ago in the war with the Nevada pack. The fight was over our territory, California. Nevada wanted to take it over. Rena and I were in the fight, too, but we were the lucky ones. Our mother was one of the best and strongest fighters our pack had. She died trying to make sure Rena and I stayed alive. She never wanted us to be in the fight at all, but our father insisted that it would teach us. We won the fight, but it took a lot of lives. After that, I learned everything I could about fighting so I wouldn't have to be protected, I could protect others.

All of the guys arrived in a stretch limo that they rented for the night. Tasha took pictures of us with our dates before she let us leave. We went out for dinner in the best restaurant in town. There were a lot of other couples eating there before prom, too. After we were finished, we got back into the limo and headed for the school.

We could hear music as we entered the building. Once we got into the gym, I was shocked. What had at first been a gym decorated with the school colors, banners, and various sport posters had been transformed into a club. There was a dance floor and colored lights, balloons, streamers, and even a DJ. The music wasn't the cheesy kind that plays in movie proms; some of it was actually the kind of music I listened to. Zander immediately whisked me away to dance, and the others started dancing, too.

"You look extremely beautiful tonight," Zander said, causing me to smile up at him.

"You look pretty handsome yourself," I replied.

We danced together for a while, until everyone decided to switch dance partners. We did this a few times, and then we all danced in a big group. When a heavy metal song came on, all of us girls, and Mike, started head banging while our dates just laughed at us. After a while, we found a couple of empty tables and sat down for a little while, joking around and talking. We didn't sit for long though. A really crazy sounding song that I had never heard before in my life started playing and Damien dragged us all back out to the dance floor. At some point, Zander and I were able to escape his crazy dancing and went back to our table. He made me sit down while he went to get us some refreshments. After a few minutes, he came back with two bottles of soda and a couple candy bars. We just sat there for a little while talking and laughing at our friends.

When it was time to announce prom King and Queen, I started laughing hysterically, remembering Shorty and I sneaking into the office to change the votes. Zander looked at me and smirked. I had a feeling that he knew what I did. I looked back to the dance floor and met Shorty's eyes. He was laughing just as much as I was. A few people started staring at us. A teacher walked up on stage and was handed an envelope.

"Your prom King is," she hesitated, looking a bit shocked, "Damien Kaynes." Damien's face immediately turned beet red as he walked up on stage. He finally realized what Shorty and I were laughing at and glared at us as we kept laughing. "And your prom Queen is," the teacher hesitated even longer this time, looking down at the paper in disbelief, "Mike Laverey?" The look on Mike's face when she said his name made Shorty and I double over.

After the prom King and Queen dance, Damien and Mike came over to us, fuming, but trying not to be amused by what we had done. When Damien and Mike looked around, receiving glares from snobbish cheerleaders who most likely wanted to be queen, and football playing jocks that they could easily beat up with their werewolf strength, they couldn't contain their laughter either. They hugged Shorty and me, thanking us because they actually did have fun. We were all having such a great time. We had no idea how badly our night would end.

My first prom was over all too soon. At midnight the teachers made every one go home, already having let us stay an hour later than we were supposed to. After the limo took us all to our houses, we all got changed into comfortable clothes and met in the basement to watch movies. We didn't want our night to end yet. I decided to go to a pizza place that was open late to get us some food. I grabbed my keys and my cell phone and headed out to the truck.

It was a fifteen minute drive to the restaurant, and once I got there, I waited another fifteen minutes for my order to be ready. I paid for the pizzas and was walking away from the counter when my phone vibrated. I balanced the pizzas in one hand and took the phone out of my pocket with the other. I had a new text. Surprisingly, it was from Greg Olden, the Virginia alpha. When I flipped open my phone to read it, I froze in place and my heart stopped. I dropped the pizzas and flew out the door and into my truck. I started it and frantically sped down the highway back towards home.

The text had read,

Shauna gave them your address. They are already here, run!

-X-

Unknown

Standing in the shadows of a busted street lamp across the road, I saw a limousine pull up to their house. They must have been at prom. Thankfully, the wind was in my favor so they didn't detect my scent. As the limo drove away, I heard their laughter fade as the four silhouettes disappeared through the door. I stood there, choosing my moment carefully. About twenty minutes later, the porch light flickered on and the most beautiful girl in the world stepped outside.

Serenity.

Instead of the prom gown she was wearing previously, she was now wearing a pair of faded, baggy jeans that were held to her body with a studded belt. She also wore a black, form-fitting t-shirt with a band logo on the front. As she walked towards a truck parked in the drive way, the wind lifted her dark hair off of her shoulders. She looked like a Goddess.

I was tempted to follow her as she drove away, but I stuck to the plan though we would have to make a few changes. I raised my thumb and index finger to my lips and let out a high pitched whistle. A moment later a black van pulled around the corner and parked on the street in front of the house. My brother stepped out and walked around to the back, opening the doors to let three men jump out. I crossed the street to join them.

"So what's going on? I saw Serenity leave," my brother asked me.

"We are still going to grab the other three. You are going to take them back home. I'm going to stay here and make sure Serenity will make it to Nevada. I know she won't abandon her friends."

He nodded. "Are you ready?"

"I've been ready," I answered as I walked to the door. I skillfully picked the lock. As I opened the door, I heard a television coming from the basement. I walked through the hallway to the door beside the kitchen. Gripping the door knob, I took a deep breath before I opened the door and made my way down the small flight of stairs, my men at my heels.

Chapter Seventeen

Back to Nevada

I pulled into the drive way and put the truck in park, not bothering to turn it off. I ran to the front door and froze. It was standing wide open. I immediately caught the smell of unfamiliar werewolves. The hair on the back of my neck instantly stood on end. I was cautious as I quietly walked through the front door, not making a sound.

When I got into the living room, I saw that the couch was shoved out of place and the coffee table was flipped on its side with everything that was on it in the floor. It looked like someone had fell over the couch and hit the table. I quickly moved on to the kitchen, only to find everything in place. I was about to walk past the basement door to check the bedrooms when I saw that it was open and that I could hear the movie that we were watching still playing.

I quietly made my way down the basement stairs. When I made it to the bottom, I knew that my sister and friends were gone. There was popcorn all over the floor and overturned cans of soda. The black curtain separating the pool table and game area from the movie area was torn down. One picture on the wall was crooked, and another was lying on the floor with the glass shattered. What worried me most though was the blood spattered on the pale carpet. After making sure no one was hiding in the basement, I threw all caution to the wind and ran up the stairs and checked all of the bedrooms and bathrooms. I even checked the pool and back yard.

As soon as I walked back into the house I started to panic. Then my phone started vibrating in my pocket again. I was getting a call from a private number. I quickly answered.

"Hello?" You could clearly hear the fear and worry in my voice.

"Hello, Serenity, are you worried about your friends?" An unfamiliar voice asked me pleasantly.

"Where are they?!" I screamed into the phone.

"Calm down, they're fine. For now."

"Please don't hurt them," I begged.

"I won't hurt Rena. You and your sister are needed for Nevada to combine with the California pack. But Zane and Zander, however, they are wanted dead. If you do exactly as I say, maybe you can save them. If you don't, they *will* die, and I may be forced to then hurt your sister."

"I'll do whatever you tell me. Just don't hurt any of them."

"Smart girl. Now, you are to come to Nevada. Once you make it into the state, send a text to your sister's cell phone. I will contact you when I receive it. If you call the cops, I will kill them." The man laughed menacingly. "Stop pacing, you will wear a path into your nice carpet."

I stopped dead in my tracks. "How did you know I was pacing?" I asked him as I frantically looked around.

"You won't be able to see me, so you might as well stop looking." He laughed again. "I am watching you from a safe distance, don't worry, I'm not in the house." I snorted. Like I would believe him. I listened intently to my surroundings, making sure I was alone. But then I remembered the blood.

"Whose blood is downstairs in the basement?" I asked him, not really wanting to know the answer.

"That blood belongs to your precious Zander." He let out yet another menacing laugh. "It was so touching when he attacked me, demanding to know where you were." My heart dropped. I made a promise to myself that I was going to kill the man who hurt Zander. I hung up on the man and ran to my room.

I grabbed a duffel bag and threw a few changes of clothes and all of my money into it, considering I was going to have to drive across the country again. And then I got an idea. I didn't have to go and face them alone. I could get my friends to help me rescue them.

I ran out to my truck. Before I got in, I checked the bed and the backseat, making sure there was no one else in the truck with me. I got in and started it. I was headed to Damien's house first. I prayed that someone would answer the door, because my best friend slept like the dead.

When I made it there, I got out of the truck and ran to the front porch. I started banging on the front door. After a few minutes, I was sure no one was going to answer, and I was about to call Damien's cell when Tasha opened the door looking irritated and in a silk robe. When she saw that it was me she looked confused for a moment. Then she saw my tear streaked face and pulled me in the house.

"Tasha, I need yours and Damien's help." I explained everything to her about Rena and I being runaways and why Zander and Zane were wanted dead. Then I told her that they had been kidnapped and what I was supposed to do. She loved Rena, Zander, and Zane, so she agreed to help me. As she went back to her room to get dressed and pack some clothes, she told me to go wake up Damien. Mike was also here staying in one of the guest rooms for the night.

I ran up the stairs and into Damien's room. He was sleeping with his head buried under the pillows and was snoring like a lawn mower. If it weren't for the situation that I was in, I would have found this hilarious. I jumped up onto his bed and shook him awake. At first, I couldn't get him to wake up; he was mumbling something about cookies. So I unburied his head and slapped him across the face. He immediately jolted awake.

At first he was really mad, but when I told him what was going on, he was instantly worried. He hurried out of bed and went to wake up Mike. They both agreed to help, too, so while they packed some clothes, I walked down stairs. I pulled my phone out of my pocket and scrolled down the contact list for Shorty's number. I had to call a couple times before he answered, still half asleep. I told him everything, and before I even asked for his help, he asked me where I wanted him to meet me. I told him to come to Damien's house and to bring some clothes with him.

As soon as we hung up, I dialed the number of Greg Olden.

"Hello?" He answered on the third ring.

"Its Serenity," I told him. "They took Rena, Zane, and Zander."

"What are you going to do?" He asked me.

"The man who called me said to come to Nevada. I'm going to rescue them."

"You aren't going alone are you?" He asked me, worried.

"No. A few friends are coming with me to help. Do you know what we can do to stay safe once we save them?"

He sighed. "I could get in a lot of trouble for telling you this. The only thing I can think of for you to do is for you and your sister to marry Zander and Zane. If you do, you can't be forced to marry someone else, and Zander and Zane would be safe, too. No one can harm the mates of an alpha or even a future alpha. And since you and your sister are your father's only children, one or both of you will become alpha one day."

I was in shock. Marriage? That's what we wanted to get away from. But I wouldn't mind marrying Zander one day, so if it could save him, I was willing.

"I'm sorry I can't help you more, Serenity," he told me, "but you are a very strong and determined werewolf. I believe you can do it."

"Thank you Greg, that really means a lot to me. If we make it out alive, I am going to do something to repay you for all of your help."

He chuckled. "That's not necessary, but good luck and I want to know how everything turns out."

"I'll make sure to tell you if I don't die." We hung up and as soon as I put my phone in my pocket, there was a knock at the door.

I walked over and looked through the peep hole before opening the door for Shorty, and hugging him tightly.

"Thank you," I said. He just hugged me back, and then followed me into the kitchen. Shorty and I were the last ones there.

"I'm really sorry to involve you all in this," I said to all of them. "I just can't do it alone."

Tasha walked up to me and pulled me into a hug.

"You don't have to be sorry, sweetie," she told me. "We love them, too. We wouldn't dream of letting you get thrown to the wolves alone." We all laughed a little at her little pun.

Soon, we were all climbing into my truck, with Shorty, Damien, and Mike in the back and Tasha in the passenger seat. We stopped back at my house on the way out of town so I could run in and get all four of our old IDs and Rena's GPS. After I set our destination, I drove off... back to Nevada.

-X-

Unknown

"Stop pacing, you will wear a path into your nice carpet." Back in the shadows across the street, I could see through the front window of the house. She stopped right in my line of vision. Her head whipped around back and forth, trying to find out where I was.

"How did you know I was pacing?"

"You won't be able to see me, so you might as well stop looking," I answered with a laugh. "I am watching you from a safe distance, don't worry, I'm not in the house." I heard her snort. She didn't believe me. I saw her slightly cock her head to the side, listening. Satisfied, she asked me another question.

"Who's blood is downstairs in the basement?"

"That blood belongs to your precious Zander," I told her with another laugh. "It was so touching when he attacked me, demanding to know where you were."

I heard the click as she hung up and rushed out of the living room. I walked out of the shadows and to the next street where my car was parked. Getting in, I pulled my cell phone back out of my pocket and made a call to the airport, booking the next flight back to Nevada.

CHAPTER EIGHTEEN

Craving for Blood

While we were driving, we came up with a plan. I was going to do whatever the man told me, and they were going to follow my scent. Once we found out where our friends were being held, we were going to attack. Shorty had three swords called katanas, and he was going to use them before he phased. We all were going to try to do what we could before we had to phase, so we could hopefully keep our clothes. As soon as we could, we were going to get out of there and explain to Rena, Zane, and Zander what we could do. We were going straight to Las Vegas. I had to make sure that they all agreed so no one would have to get married against their will, but I was almost positive that they would want to do it so we all could be safe. And it didn't hurt that we were in love with the people we were going to marry. It probably would have happened at some point any way, just not like this.

All of us were going to be wearing black clothing so it would be easier to hide; it would be dark when we got to Nevada. It took a few days to get there, but we took turns driving so we would only have to stop for food and gas. Once we passed the border into Nevada,

I pulled over at a gas station. After we got gas and everyone was back in the truck, I pulled my phone off the travel charger and sent a text to Rena's cell phone saying what city we were in. Soon after, my phone vibrated, signaling an incoming call. I told everyone to be quiet. After taking a deep breath, I answered the phone and put it on speaker so that they could hear what was going on.

"Hello?"

"I'm glad you finally made it. Your friends were getting restless."

"If you hurt them, I swear, I'll make you regret it," I told him menacingly.

"Serenity, you really aren't in the position to threaten me."

"Oh it's not a threat, it's a promise." He laughed at my threat. "Just tell me where to go," I said, irritated.

He gave me an address and Tasha entered it into the GPS.

"Get here soon, Serenity, your friends are waiting." I heard a scream and then he hung up. I couldn't move. Tasha took the phone from my hand and pressed end; no one made a sound.

"T-that was R-Rena," I stuttered. Damien patted my shoulder.

"Don't worry Serenity. She's safe, they need you both," he told me. I shook my head.

"I'm okay," I said to him and turned back to the steering wheel and started the truck. "Now I just have another reason to kill him. When we get in there, no one touch him... he's mine," I growled.

I pulled out of the gas station and followed the instruction the GPS gave me. About five miles before our destination, I pulled over at another gas station. It was almost midnight, so it was dark enough for us to change into the black clothes. Shorty was already in black. He was wearing a ninja outfit with his katanas in a holder on his back. *Afro ninja,* I thought and let out a little giggle. He gave me a curious look, but I just shook my head. I took my clothes out of my bag as Tasha did the same. We both went into the women's restroom and Damien and Mike went into the men's. I quickly changed into a plain black tank top, black skinny jeans, and a pair of black converse low tops.

Tasha was wearing a black t-shirt with medium length sleeves, black skinny jeans, and black on black high tops. When we left the restroom, Damien and Mike were already by the truck, talking to Shorty. When I saw their t-shirts, I had to laugh. They were both black, but Damien's shirt said "That's What She Said" and Mike's shirt said "Epic Fail" with an arrow pointing to where Damien was standing. When Tasha read their shirts, she started laughing too. They just smiled.

After we were back in the truck, we went over the plan again. When everyone knew what we were going to do, I started the truck and pulled out onto the road and followed the GPS.

I pulled up to a big fence. Behind it was a mansion. I immediately knew where we were. This was the house of the Nevada alpha. Everyone except me got out of the truck and went to hide behind some bushes. I pulled out my phone and sent a text to Rena's cell phone.

I'm in front of the fence. Soon, I got a text back.

It will open. Pull in and go to the back door.

I wasn't going to pull into the drive way, I'm not stupid. If the truck was on the other side of the fence, we would never get away after it closed. I opened the glove box and got out a pocket knife and put it in my back pocket. I got out of the truck as the gate opened and walked through, before it closed behind me. After I was half way up the drive way, I heard my friends climbing the fence. When I looked back, I saw that they were staying hidden behind trees so they wouldn't be seen from the house.

When I got to the back of the house, there was a werewolf in human form waiting for me at the door. He was huge! He was around 6'5 and really muscular. He had short blond hair and icy blue eyes. I climbed the stairs onto the porch and looked at him. "Are you the man from the phone?" I asked him. He shook his head and told me to come into the house. I went in and stopped inside of the door. When I looked around, I saw that I was in a kitchen. The man closed the door and locked it. Then he walked ahead of me and motioned for me to follow. I pretended to trip and catch my balance on the door, unlocking it in the process so my friends could get in. When the man turned to see what the noise was, he gave me a skeptical look.

"What?" I asked. "Can't there be one clumsy werewolf in the world?" I waved my hands forward. "Let's go". He rolled his eyes and kept walking. As we walked through the house, I made sure that I remembered how to get back to the door. I didn't see or hear anyone else except for us, but I could smell other werewolves.

He led me to a door and opened it, revealing stairs leading to the basement. He walked down the stairs and I followed, leaving the door open. Once down the stairs, I saw Rena, Zander, and Zane on their knees in the floor with their hands tied behind their backs. There were two men pointing guns at them, three men standing against the back wall, two guys were standing at the foot of the stairs, and two younger looking guys were sitting at a little table in the middle of the room, playing cards.

After I took in how many people we were up against, I immediately ran to Zander and threw my arms around his neck, hugging him. "I'm so sorry," I told him, tears running down my cheeks.

"It's okay, it's not your fault," he said to me, trying to calm me down.

I gave him a little smile. "I love you."

"I love you, too," he said back to me.

I hugged him again, whispering in his ear so no one else would hear. "Damien, Mike, Tasha, and Shorty are here, too. We are gonna get you out." I hugged Zane and Rena next, telling them the same. Then I stood up, facing the werewolves in front of me.

One of the guys sitting at the table stood and walked towards me.

"Hello, Serenity, nice to finally see you." I immediately recognized him as the man from the phone.

"I wish I could say the same," I said, glaring at him. He laughed. "So you know who I am, who are you?"

He smirked, "You don't know?" I shook my head. He pointed to the guy still sitting at the table. "That is my brother Matt, and I am Trevor Krate, the man you were supposed to marry."

CHAPTER NINETEEN

Blood Bath

I stared at him in shock. The last time I had seen him was in a picture about two years ago and he and his brother were total nerds. Now they were really muscular and kind of good looking. They looked like the kind of guys who would be popular jocks in school. I still didn't regret not marrying him, because for one, he was obviously psychotic with the kidnapping and all, and two, he definitely wasn't my type. I didn't like preps or jocks. I liked guys like Zander.

"You're Trevor Krate?" I asked in a disbelieving tone. He nodded. I just snorted and shook my head with a smirk.

"What's so funny?"

"Nothing much, just the fact that you both were complete nerds the last time I saw you." He looked a little mad for a second, and then he smiled.

"And what do you think now?" He asked.

"You're hot now." He grinned back at me. "But I still wouldn't marry you," and his grin disappeared.

"And why not?"

"Are you really stupid enough to have to ask? You are obviously crazy. You kidnapped my sister and my friends, and you're arrogant. I want to marry someone I love, and you are so not my type at all." After I finished, he looked furious.

"And that idiot over there is your type?"

I smiled. "Yes. I happen to be in love with that idiot."

"Oh well, he and his brother are going to die, and you are going to marry me anyway."

I rolled my eyes. "You think so, huh?" He just nodded arrogantly. "Well, not gonna happen." I punched him in the face as hard as I could and he fell to the ground. I then turned around and knocked the gun out of one of the guys hands that was about to shoot at me. I hit him in the side of the face, and when he fell, I hit him in the head with the gun, knocking him out. Zander had brought his legs around and kicked the other gun man in the back of his knee, making him fall so I wouldn't get shot. I heard Tasha, Damien, Mike, and Shorty coming down the stairs. The other men in the room were coming toward us.

I pointed the gun at Trevor. "Don't move," I told him. All of the other men froze, too. Damien hurried over to the man that Zander knocked over and picked up his gun, pointing at the men in front of us. I handed my gun to Mike and walked over to Zander, pulling the knife out of my back pocket. I opened it and cut the rope that was binding Zander's wrists together. I then cut Rena and Zane's ropes, too. Before I knew what was going on, everyone was fighting. I had no idea how they got the guns away from Mike and Damien, but they were lying across the room. I was running towards them when someone grabbed my arm.

It was Trevor. He swung back his arm and hit me in the jaw before I could block. I didn't fall, I can take a punch, but dropped the knife instead. I tackled him, both of us hitting the ground. I rolled over on top of him, about to hit him, but before I could, he grabbed my wrist, only inches from his face. He threw me off, rolling over me. We wrestled around like that for a few moments. Finally when I rolled over him, I got his arms pinned under my knees. I just started hitting him in the face over and over, thinking about Zander's blood in my basement and Rena's terrified scream on the phone.

At some point, he lost consciousness, but I kept hitting him until someone came up behind me, grabbing me around the waist and by my hair, dragging me off Trevor. I was so angry, I couldn't help it. I phased. I must have shocked the man that grabbed me, because he let go and I hit the floor. I turned and lunged at him, biting his wrist hard, disgusting blood pouring into my mouth. The man let out a scream and started hitting me with his other fist. I growled and let go, only to lunge again, this time getting a death grip on his throat. I closed my mouth completely on his neck and jerked backwards, ripping it open. He clutched at it, blood squirting out from between his fingers. He choked, blood also pouring from his mouth as he fell to the ground.

I turned and looked around as I shook out of my clothes, hoping they weren't completely ruined. Shorty was doing well with his katanas; I could see at least three people he had killed already. Rena was fighting Matt. He was pretty messed up, but I could tell that he got a few hits in on Rena. Zander was fighting with two men alongside Tasha, who was fighting a man who looked like he was going to pass out at any moment. There weren't many people in wolf form other than me. Zane had phased and was fighting three other wolves. There were a lot of dead bodies lying around, but all of my friends were alive.

There were a lot more people in the basement fighting than there had been when the fight first started. A few more people came running down the basement stairs. I ran at them, hitting a woman in the middle of her chest. She was flung backwards, hitting her head on the concrete wall. She died instantly. I wasn't paying attention and a wolf jumped at me, grabbing my tail between his teeth, causing me to howl in pain. I swung myself around and it hit the wall, letting go. I attacked it as soon as its teeth unclenched from my tail. I tried biting at the wolves face unsuccessfully. I instead grabbed its ear, ripping it off. It howled in agony, and while it was distracted, I grabbed its throat. I didn't get the chance to tear it out, because I heard a gunshot. I let go and whipped my head around. I saw a man firing at Zander and Zane. He just barely missed Zane; the bullet flew right past his ear.

I took off running at the man as he fired at Zander. Thankfully, he was fast, so he pulled the body of the man he was fighting in front of him, and it took the bullet. As he fired again, I hit him in the side, knocking him over. The bullet hit the ceiling. I tore into his arm with my teeth, making him drop the gun. I could tell that this man was squeamish and weak, because he passed out quickly from the pain.

I let go and turned around just in time to see Shorty ripping his sword out of the last man. He looked around and grinned, counting all of the bodies in the huge, bloody basement. "Damn, were good, son!" He said with a laugh. "Just the eight of us killed nineteen werewolves!"

I barked in agreement, trotting over to my clothes and phasing back into my human form, not really caring who saw me naked at that point. I quickly dressed and turned around to see that Zane was already dressed and standing next to everyone else. I started to walk over to them when Zander looked behind me and shouted my name. I reacted too late and hit the ground, face first. I looked behind me to see that Trevor was conscious again and that he grabbed my ankle. He started to pull me towards him. When I was close enough, I used the leg that he wasn't holding and kicked him in the face to make him let go.

I quickly got up and jumped at him, again straddling his chest.

For once, to my good luck, my knife was laying right beside his head. I picked it up and stared into his black eyes as he struggled under me, glaring. I raised the knife, about to stab him when his arrogant look stopped me. He snorted. "You don't have the guts, Serenity. You can't do it."

"Oh really?" I asked. I motioned for him to look around. "I killed quite a few of these people, Trevor. What makes you any different? I completely despise you."

He rolled his eyes, though I could tell that he wasn't as sure anymore. "You won't kill me."

This time it was my turn to snort. "Watch me," I growled, as I plunged the knife into his throat. I watched with grim satisfaction as the blood gushed from his throat and poured out of his mouth as he choked on it. "Not so arrogant now are you?" I asked as I could see the life draining from his eyes. I stood and looked at my friends. They stared at me in shock. "What?" I asked. "I told him I was going to kill him."

We ran out of the house and climbed the fence, getting in the truck and speeding off down the road, Mike, Damien, and I riding in the bed. We headed for a gas station so we could clean up and change clothes. Damien let Zane and Zander borrow some clothes and I did the same for Rena. Once we were ready to leave, I stopped Zane, Zander and Rena so I could explain to them the only way we could stay safe for sure.

"Um, Rena, I know this is going to be hard to hear since it's the reason we ran away it the first place, but," I hesitated. "Greg Olden said that the only way he could think of for us to stay safe is for you, Zane, Zander and me to get married." I explained why and all the little details about Vegas.

They all looked at me in shock for a moment, and then Zane broke into a grin. "If Rena doesn't care its fine with me," he said loudly, picking her up and swinging her around in a circle.

She squealed and then let out a giggle. "Zane is the only man on this Earth that I want to marry," she said as he put her down. She kissed him, and then they walked toward the truck, Zane's arm around my sister's waist, giving Zander and I a little bit of privacy.

He just looked into my eyes for a few moments and then smiled at me. He got down on one knee and took my hand in his. "Serenity, will you marry me?" He asked. I looked at him for a moment, trying to assess if he was serious or not.

"Do you really want to marry me?" I asked him, suddenly afraid that he was only going to do it to avoid death.

"Yes, Serenity, I want to marry you. I love you more than anything." And I could see in his eyes that he was sincere.

"Yes!" I shouted, ecstatic. He stood up and pulled me into a breath taking kiss. When he pulled back, he smiled at me, happily.

"Let's go to Las Vegas, my beautiful fiancé," he said to me, and we walked hand in hand to our truck.

CHAPTER TWENTY

Preparations

We stopped at a hotel for the night. It was a five star hotel and was absolutely gorgeous inside. Tasha used her credit card and got two master suites, one for the boys and one for the girls, plus Mike. "I don't care that you're getting married tomorrow," Tasha said when Rena objected, wanting to stay with Zane. "You know my feelings about sex before marriage, and frankly, I don't trust any of you." I bit my lip to hold in a laugh when I saw Mike's face. He clearly wanted to stay with Damien.

Tasha handed a key to Shorty as he and Damien walked over to the elevator. Zane and Zander stayed for a moment to give Rena and me a quick kiss before for following after them. Tasha, Rena, Mike, and I went to a little shop inside the hotel because we all were seriously craving some candy. I grabbed so many things that Rena had to help me carry it. "You are gonna put yourself into a sugar coma," she giggled.

"It's not like I plan on eating it all tonight," I told her. She just rolled her eyes because she could see right through me. I did, in fact, plan on eating most of it tonight. I figured I would indulge a little.

Or a lot. I felt I deserved it, considering what we went through. When I looked at all of the candy I started to reconsider, but then thought, *What the hell, I'll just go for a jog in the morning*, and grabbed a soda, too, though I knew that I would not be jogging.

We dropped all of the sugary goodness on the counter and Rena walked back over to where Tasha and Mike were already waiting for me. The woman behind the register just looked at me in shock before starting to ring up my purchases. I bought a soda, a bag of hard candy, five candy bars, a bag of spicy fries, and a bag of gummy worms. She gave me a total and I pulled my wallet out of my pocket while she put the food into a bag. When I handed her the money I heard her let out a quiet gasp. She was staring at my arm, so I looked down at myself to see massive bruises starting to form. The woman looked at me questioningly as she handed me my change. I just shook my head, taking the money, and grabbing my bag. We followed Tasha to the elevator and went upstairs.

When we made it inside our room, I looked around in shock. It was a massive suite. It had a full kitchen, two bathrooms, a huge living room, and three bedrooms. There was a flat screen T.V. in every bedroom and in the living room. Our bags were already sitting in the room, thanks to the bellhop. We decided that Tasha and Mike would have their own rooms, and Rena and I would share one.

Rena and I moved our bags into our room so that we could change into some comfy pajamas, and then went back into the living room to sit with Tasha and Mike. We watched T.V. for a while and I opened my bag of hard candy. I threw the blue ones at Rena, the purple ones at Tasha, and the green ones at Mike. I only liked the red and pink ones. After an hour or two, Tasha drifted into her room, telling us that we should get some sleep because we had a big day ahead of us tomorrow.

Soon after, the rest of us went to bed. Rena was asleep almost instantly, but my mind was wandering too much to sleep. I got out of bed and pulled on some shoes. I grabbed my bag of candy and the room key, and then walked out the door. At the end of the hall way, there was a door leading out onto a balcony. When I walked outside, I saw Zane sitting at a little table, looking up at the stars. I pulled out a chair next to him and sat down. "Why aren't you in bed?" I asked him.

"Couldn't sleep, you?"

"My mind is way too full to sleep." I poured out all of my candy onto the table. Zane looked down at it and chucked. I smiled at him. "Want some?"

"Sure," he said, as we both picked up a candy bar.

"So what do you think about getting married tomorrow?" I asked him.

He smiled. "I'm excited. I wasn't planning on doing it this soon, but your sister is the only one I would ever want to marry."

"You're good for her. You're also the only guy she has ever opened up to. I don't know why, but she tends to shy away from men, sometimes, even Damien and Mike. I'm glad she has found someone she loves and trusts enough to marry."

He smiled at me. "You are really good for my brother, too. I've never seen him so happy in my entire life until he met you. When he first saw you, his whole face lit up, like love at first sight. I'm glad he picked you to be my new sister. And if you ever need anything, or want me to beat someone up for you, I'll be there for you. I already think of you as my little sister."

What he said made me feel extremely happy. "Thank you, Zane. You're an awesomely, awesome big brother."

He raised an eyebrow. "Awesomely, awesome?"

I laughed a little. "I made it up. It's the most awesome you can get in my book," I answered. He chuckled. "Well I should get back to bed before Rena comes looking for me. She would throw me off the balcony if she caught me trying to steal her man," I joked and he laughed again.

"Good night," he told me, giving me a hug.

"'Night."

I walked back to our suite and climbed back into bed, finally able to get some sleep.

-X-

Tasha woke me up way too early the next morning. "You need to get up. We're in a hurry if you and Rena are going to get married tonight." We heard a crash in the kitchen and then we could smell smoke. "Rena is in the kitchen attempting to make us some breakfast. Maybe you should go and save the food while it's still edible." We heard another crash, and I hurried out of bed and into the kitchen. I was shocked when I saw the stove. It was on fire and Rena was beating at it with a dish towel. I rushed over and grabbed the towel from her.

"Rena, get some wat—" I started to say, but she wasn't paying attention. She opened a cabinet and pulled out the container of salt. "No Rena, water!" But I was too late. She had poured out the entire container of salt onto the stove, successfully putting out the fire. "Or just use the salt," I muttered under my breath. Rena looked at me a moment and then started laughing hysterically. Soon, I was laughing, too. I glanced into the pot on the stove. "Rena, this is water. How the hell did you set the stove on fire?" I asked her, still laughing. "I taught you to cook myself." I was a pretty good cook. I planned on going to culinary school after a few years of college.

Rena looked guilty. "I was texting Zane," she mumbled.

"Rena, if you're going to cook, keep your phone out of the kitchen, okay?" She nodded. "And guess what? Since you didn't listen to me about the water, considering the salt just makes a huge mess, you get to clean it up while I take a shower, and after everyone is dressed, I'll take everyone out for breakfast." She just rolled her eyes and started to clean up as I walked out.

I took a quick shower and got dressed. When Rena was finished getting ready, we went out to the truck. Tasha had already talked to Zane and Zander and gave them our old IDs with our real names on them so that our marriage would actually be legal. They were going to call a cab to do whatever they were going to do, and Shorty and Mike were going with them. Damien wanted to come with us because he wanted to help us find dresses. Rena and I weren't allowed to see Zander and Zane until the weddings tonight. Tasha told them to find a chapel and book our weddings.

After we stopped to get something to eat, we went to a few different stores until we found dresses that everyone approved of. They were both really simple and about knee length. Both were white, but Rena's dress had a black ribbon around the waist. I questioned Rena about the black ribbon, but she just sheepishly changed the subject. When we got accessories, Tasha made sure we had everything. For something blue, we both bought white gold earrings with sapphires. Tasha let me borrow a beautiful white gold bracelet, and she let Rena borrow black bangles, though I had no idea how she thought to bring them with her in the first place. We both bought new white heels, and I wore the necklace that Zander gave me for my birthday as something old. Rena wore the locket that our father gave her for her thirteenth birthday. Tasha just bought herself a plain black dress.

After shopping, we went to a salon. Tasha told them what to do with our hair, makeup, and nails. We weren't allowed to peek until everything was finished. When we were finally allowed to see ourselves, I was shocked at how beautiful I looked. My dark hair was curled and partially pinned up on top of my head. I wasn't wearing much makeup. In fact, you couldn't even tell I was wearing any, but my skin looked flawless. Rena's hair was pinned up almost exactly like it was for prom. Her makeup was also very natural looking.

We went back to the hotel room. Damien called Zander to find out what chapel we were supposed to go to later. Tasha refused to let Rena and I eat because she thought that we would ruin our faces. Then she and Damien ate right in front of us. Rena and I made a pact to have revenge, we were so hungry. Soon, it was time to get dressed. Tasha was hesitant to let Damien help at first, but when he reminded her that he was gay, she just rolled her eyes and nodded. Once we were finished, we went back to the truck and Damien drove us to a little chapel in the center of the city. We walked inside and were immediately shown to a room where we could wait and make last minute touch ups on our appearances.

When my name was called, I was suddenly really nervous. I was about to marry the man I loved. I was going to spend the rest of my life with him. Tasha and Rena went out to take their seats. Damien had agreed as my best friend to walk me down the aisle. After he had me calmed down enough, we waited for the wedding march to start, so I could start the rest of my life as Serenity Noonan.

CHAPTER TWENTY-ONE

The Wedding

When the wedding march began, I almost started hyperventilating. I even thought that I would forget the vows that we chose to rehearse as we were waiting.

"Just take a deep breath, Serenity. It will be fine. You're going to spend the rest of your life, married to Zander. You two love each other, and he's a great guy. If you weren't about to marry him and I wasn't in love with Mike, I might have taken a swing at him myself," Damien said to me with a smile. I giggled at his confession. I was suddenly more confident and I had a smile on my face. Damien and I walked out the door and started down the aisle.

Tasha, Mike, and Shorty were standing in front of one of the pews, watching me with smiles as I walked. The minister was standing at the end of the aisle. Rena was beside him as my maid of honor, and Zane was standing across from her as Zander's best man. They had smiles on their faces as they looked at each other. Finally, my eyes met Zander's. He was standing at the end of the aisle waiting for me with a grin of pure joy lighting up his eyes. I felt my expression matched his. When we finished our walk, Damien placed my hand in Zander's and kissed my cheek, then went over and sat down by Mike.

The music came to a slow end as the minister began to speak.

"It is one of life's richest surprises when the accidental meeting of two life paths lead them to proceed together along the common path as husband and wife. It is one of life's finest experiences when a casual relationship grows into a permanent bond of love. This meeting and this growth bring us together today." Zander and I exchanged loving glances. Our meeting was indeed accidental. But we were both glad we had found each other.

"Zander Noonan and Serenity Landon, will you take vows here before us which symbolize the manifested vows you have already made and will continue to make to each other throughout your lives?"

"I will," we said in unison.

"I, Zander Noonan, take you, Serenity Landon, as my friend and love, beside me and apart from me, in laughter and in tears, in conflict and tranquility, asking that you be no other than yourself, loving what I know of you, trusting what I do not yet know, in all the ways that life may find us." He said his vows with a smile. Then it was my turn.

"I, Serenity Landon, take you, Zander Noonan, as my friend and love, beside me and apart from me, in laughter and in tears, in conflict and tranquility, asking that you be no other than yourself, loving what I know of you, trusting what I do not yet know, in all the ways that life may find us." I didn't stutter or stumble once. I said the vows perfectly because that was what I truly felt in my heart.

The minister started speaking again. "The circle is the symbol of the sun, earth, and universe. It is the symbol of peace. Let these rings be the symbol of unity and peace in which your two lives are joined in one unbroken circle. Wherever you go, return unto one another and to your togetherness." *Rings?* I didn't know that we were giving each other rings now. I thought that we would wait until we had more time to get them, but Zander was always full of surprises.

Zane handed Zander a ring and Rena handed me one as well. The ring that she handed me was the white gold band that I saw in a shop window while we were shopping. I had planned on going to buy it before we left, because I didn't think that I would have time before the wedding. I was wondering where Rena had gone off to with my wallet while we were getting Tasha's dress. She must have been buying it. I looked at the ring and I saw the beautiful script written in side, it said, *I Love You.*

Zander took my left hand in his, "I give you this ring to wear upon your hand as a symbol of our union and eternal love." He slipped a beautiful white gold ring onto my finger. Three bands wrapped around and met in the center at a one carat diamond. The middle band had small diamonds going down the sides. It was the most beautiful ring I had ever seen in my life.

As I slipped his ring onto his left hand, I said, "I give you this ring to wear upon your hand as a symbol of our union and eternal love," Zander smiled down at me.

The minister began to speak again. "You are mature people who have established individual patterns of living. Yet you have found not only a need for companionship, but the satisfaction of that need in each others' company. It is this love, based upon a responsible understanding that will aid you in creating out of your two lives, a marriage and a happiness you will share together. Stand fast in hope and confidence, believing in yourself and believing in each other. In as much as you two have come before your friends and family and have declared your love and devotion to each other, I now announce you to them as husband and wife. You may kiss the bride."

Zander bent down and captured my lips in a breathtaking kiss. If he hadn't been holding me up, I think my knees would have given out. When he pulled away and faced us toward our friends, the minister said, "Mr. and Mrs. Zander Noonan."

"I like the sound of that," I said, looking up at my husband. He just smiled down at me and pulled me closer.

Zander and his brother switched places to get ready for Zane and Rena's wedding. Rena asked me to walk her down the aisle and I obliged. We went to the doors and the wedding march began again. As I walked my big sister down the aisle, I squeezed her hand. She looked at me, and we smiled at each other. I put her hand in Zane's and stepped to the side. The minister handed Zander and I their rings. As the ceremony began, I wasn't paying much attention.

Zander and I were staring into each others' eyes the entire time. When I handed Rena the ring, I didn't break eye contact. Before I knew it, the ceremony was over. My husband took my hand as our friends congratulated us. Soon, we were heading out the door. When we stepped outside, I noticed that my truck was gone and a stretch limo was parked in its place. The limo had a banner that said, *Just Married*, on the back with streamers flowing down.

"Um... What happened to my truck?" I asked.

"I had it taken back to the hotel," Tasha told me. "Tonight is your wedding night. You deserve to ride in style. I have also already planned the reception which we are going to now. You and Zander, and Rena and Zane now have your own rooms in the hotel so you can be alone," Tasha winked at me as my face turned beet red. Damien chuckled at my reaction.

"Mike and I should get our own room, too," he told his aunt with a smirk.

"Nice try, Damien," she replied, rolling her eyes.

"It was worth a shot," he said, defeated, making me laugh. We all climbed into the limo. Tasha told the driver where to go and then sat down next to Shorty. From beside her seat, she picked up a box. She pulled out two white sashes that said Bride in black letters. She handed one to me, and one to Rena. Then she handed Zander and

Zane two black baseball caps that said Groom in white letters. We all put them on as soon we arrived at a club.

Tasha walked us right up to the bouncer. "We're here for the private party," she told him. "This is Serenity and Zander, and Rena and Zane."

He nodded at us, and mumbled, "Congratulations," and let us in. We followed Tasha into a private room, and inside I saw another banner. This one said, *Congratulations Newly Weds.* There was a long table in the middle of the room with a black table cloth, and enough food to feed an army. Black and white streamers and balloons decorated the room.

"Your Aunt works fast, son," Shorty said to Damien,

"Yeah, she does," he replied. "And if you think this is a lot, you should see the birthday parties she throws." Shorty just shook his head.

We all ate and then went out into the main club and danced for a while. At some point, I saw Shorty, Zane, and Rena disappear out the back door.

"Do you think that they will ever quit?" I asked Zander. I knew that they were all going out to smoke.

"Probably not," he replied with a smirk. I saw Tasha watching them leave with narrowed eyes. She was about to go after them when Damien held her back.

"They just got married, Mom, let them celebrate." Tasha looked at him in a mix of surprise and joy. Damien had never called her Mom before. I knew that she had wanted him to, but he wouldn't. She threw her arms around him in a hug.

"I love you, Damien," she told him, letting one joyful tear escape.

"I love you, too, Mom," he replied, hugging her back.

I had a smile on my face. I loved seeing families happy. Even after what he did, I had to admit to myself that I missed my Dad. I knew that Rena did too, even though they weren't that close. I made a promise to myself to go and visit him soon, considering that now he couldn't make me marry Trevor. I would tell him everything that happened and forgive him. I hoped that he would be able to forgive me, too.

The party was over too soon. We rode in the limo to a gas station across from the hotel, and told the driver that he could leave us here and we would walk to the hotel. He left and Zander and I walked inside. I had begged Tasha to let us stop so I could get more candy. Everyone else decided to wait outside. Zander and I picked out a lot of different candy and some soda. He paid for them and we walked outside.

We had started to walk across the parking to our friends when I heard the cries of a puppy. "Do you hear that?" I asked Zander. He nodded and listened for a moment.

"It's under that car," he told me. I handed him the bag that I was carrying.

"Go ahead and wait with everyone," I told him. "I'm going to get the puppy and try to smuggle it into the hotel to take home with us if that's okay with you." He nodded and smiled at me.

I walked over the car and crouched down beside it. When I looked under it, I saw the cutest Siberian husky puppy with beautiful blue eyes. "Come here, baby," I cooed. It hesitantly crawled over to me. I picked her up and snuggled her. I started walking back over to everyone when the puppy started squirming, wanting to get over there before me. I sat her down and she ran towards them. Mike picked her and started playing with her.

All of a sudden, I got the scent of werewolves that wasn't familiar. Too late to react, I heard a gunshot go off. I felt excruciating pain in my abdomen. I met Zander's horror filled eyes right before I collapsed. I saw everyone transform except for Mike, who was still holding the frightened puppy. With the dog in his arms, he ran over to me and dropped to his knees beside me, trying to tell me to stay awake and keep breathing.

The last thing I remember before passing out from the pain was seeing a giant ball of curly fur that reminded me of a poodle. *Was that Shorty?* Was my last conscious thought before I succumbed to the darkness.

Chapter Twenty-Two

Zander

Zander

When I heard the shot go off, I immediately knew what had happened and I was horrified. The look on my Serenity's face when the pain registered was heart breaking. I felt her pain and then some; it felt as if my heart was ripped in two. Through the pain there was a murderous rage filling my brain. I phased instantly, and as soon as my front paws hit the ground I was running. I barely noticed my friends phasing, too. "Mike, stay with Serenity, and don't let her fall asleep," Tasha told Mike right before she phased as well.

The other werewolves were all still in human form and running away from us as fast as they could. But I was faster. I lunged at the man holding the gun, the man who shot my wife. I knocked him to the ground, causing his gun to fall from his hands and slide across the concrete. He didn't get the chance to phase. I was tearing into him with my teeth and claws. I literally started ripping him to pieces. He had shot my Serenity. His pack killed my mother and father. They tried to kill me, my brother, and my new sister. *And he may have killed Serenity.* These thoughts fed my rage. I began to rip and tear even faster. Just ripping his throat out wouldn't have been satisfying enough. I had to put this man through agony.

Soon, he was torn to shreds. I looked up and saw four other wolves in human form lying dead on the ground with their throats ripped out. *I also saw a giant poodle staring at me?* 'Go help Serenity. We'll take care of the bodies.' I realized that the poodle was Shorty. I took off running back to my wife. I stopped beside my clothes and phased back to my human form. I threw on my dress pants and my dress shirt, and pulled on my shoes. I was sure my clothes were ripped, but I didn't care. I ran to her and dropped down to my knees beside Mike, who was putting pressure on the entry wound. Her white dress was soaked in crimson blood.

Every one was standing around us. I gently picked her up and hurried across the road to the truck. Shorty and I got in the back, holding Serenity. Zane and Rena got in the front with Zane driving and Tasha and Damien got into the truck bed. My brother peeled out of the parking lot, speeding to a werewolf-friendly hospital close by. While driving, he was trying to comfort Rena, who was sobbing.

Shorty opened the little window that opened to the bed so he could talk to Tasha. "Where is Mike?" He asked her.

"He's going to get a taxi so he can go put Serenity's puppy in a kennel. Zane gave him the address to the hospital so he'll meet us there."

I zoned out everything that wasn't my wife. "You are going to be okay," I murmured to her. "Just keep breathing and you will be fine. I love you, baby. Please don't leave me. Just keep breathing." Soon we were pulling into the emergency room parking lot. As soon as the truck stopped we were getting out. I rushed her through the doors. A woman behind the desk saw us come in.

"My wife has been shot," I yelled to her. She quickly picked up a phone and spoke into it. Then she walked to my side and asked what happened. After I told her everything she asked for a lot of information about her that I didn't know, so Rena answered her.

Two men came running through a set of double doors with a gurney, helping me set her down. I could already hear her heart beat weakening. The men rushed the gurney back through the doors and down the hall. They wouldn't allow me to follow.

Shorty and I went to a bathroom to clean ourselves up a bit. After we did what we could, we went to the waiting area where everyone else was sitting.

"They have her stabilized. She will be going to surgery in a little while," Rena said, her voice shaking. "The doctor said that they would tell us as soon as they had news." I nodded and sat down beside her and my brother.

"Maybe you should call your father," Tasha said to Rena. "It's not like he can do much about who you are married to now, and he does have the right to know."

Rena nodded. Damien pulled out his cell phone and handed it to her. She dialed her father's cell phone number and hesitantly pressed talk. Sitting this close to her, I could hear both sides. After three rings, I heard a sad voice. "Hello?"

"Dad?" She asked nervously.

"Oh my God, Rena? Is it really you?" He sounded relived and excited.

"Yeah, Dad, it's me."

"Where are you, baby? Are you coming home? I'm so sorry."

"Its okay, Dad. No, I'm not coming home. We are in a hospital in Nevada. Ren was shot."

"Oh no. Tell me where you are. I'll come to the hospital."

Rena gave him the address. "Are you at home, Dad?"

"No baby, I'm actually already in Nevada. I was going to tell the Krate's that the deal was off."

"Dad, whatever you do, do not go the Krate house. It isn't safe.

Come straight to the hospital. I'll explain everything when you get here. All you need to know right now is that the Krate brothers tried to kill us but we killed them first."

"How did you two accomplish that? A lot of people run with them. Did you have help?"

"Again, Dad, I'll explain when you get here. Just hurry please. There are some people I want you to meet. And I know Serenity will want to see you."

"I'm only a few miles away. I'll be there soon. I love you, Rena."

"I love you, too, dad."

She hung up the phone and looked at Shorty. "Can we go outside for a few minutes before my Dad gets here? I'm still really stressed out." He nodded and Rena and Zane followed him outside. I rolled my eyes and sat back. I could feel the tears starting to run down my cheeks. Tasha moved to the seat beside me and put her arm around my shoulder.

"She's going to be okay, Zander, don't worry. I know she'll pull through. She's a very strong girl. She wouldn't leave this world without putting up a hell of a fight." She chuckled.

"I know, but I love her so much. I can't stand even the thought of losing her."

"I love her, too, Hun. In this short time I have known her, she's like a daughter to me. And I know that she has always been like a sister to Damien." I looked over to see Damien sobbing, with tears streaming down his face.

"Speaking of Damien, it looks like he needs you right now more than I do." She glanced over at him, and then looked back to me. She pulled me in for a tight hug and then went over to try and comfort her son.

A few minutes later, Mike came into the waiting room. When he saw Damien, he rushed over to him and pulled him into a hug. They sat there holding hands and crying together. I could tell that they were in love. I couldn't be around them; it made me think of my Serenity. I got up and went down to the ground floor to find a vending machine so I could get something to drink. When I got there, I heard arguing coming from the lobby. After buying my soda, I walked down the hall to see what was going on. There was a man arguing with the same receptionist we talked to earlier when we brought Serenity in. She looked a little worried, so I decided to step in.

"Is everything alright?" I asked. She looked a little relieved. The man spoke.

"She won't tell me where my daughters are. One of them was just brought in from being shot."

"Sir, I'm sorry," she told him. "There is no one by the name of Landon here." I took a good look at the man for the first time. He had jet black hair and blue eyes. He looked almost exactly like Serenity.

"Landon?" I asked. "Are you Serenity's father?" He looked relieved.

"You know where she and Rena are?"

"Yes, Mr. Landon, I do." I told the receptionist, "I'll take him to the waiting room." She nodded. I started walking back to the elevators with Mr. Landon following. When we got inside one, I introduced myself. "I'm Zander Noonan."

"Brad Landon," he replied, shaking my hand. "Why did the receptionist lie to me about my daughters being here?"

"Um, technically, she didn't." I was suddenly really nervous to be inside a closed elevator with him. "She didn't know who you were talking about. Your daughter's last names aren't Landon anymore."

"What are you trying to say to me, boy?" I sighed. As the elevator door opened I told him the truth.

"As of a few hours ago, their last names are now Noonan. Rena just married my brother Zane and I just married Serenity."

-X-

Serenity

Beep. Beep. Beep. That beeping was starting to get on my nerves.

Beep. Beep. Beep. *What the hell is that sound?* I thought. I couldn't open my eyes to check. *Why are my eyelids so heavy? Where am I?* I could smell bleach and Lysol. *I must be in a hospital. Why is it always me in the hospital?* I groaned. I was surprised to hear it out loud. "Serenity?" I immediately recognized the voice of my sister. With a lot of effort, I opened my eyes. My vision was blurry for a few moments, but after blinking a few times, I could see her clearly.

"Rena?" I asked softly. I could feel oxygen lines running up to my nose. They were really annoying. I started to tug at them but Rena grabbed my hand and held it so I couldn't rip them out. I tried to sit up, but a jolt of pain shot through my back and abdomen. I groaned again, but this time in pain.

"Just rest, Ren. You don't want to hurt yourself again."

"What happened?" I asked her. But my memories of the day came rushing back to me.

"You were shot, Serenity."

"Of course I was. Why does all the bad stuff happen to me?" Rena giggled.

"Well it has to happen to someone so why not you?" She joked. I tried to laugh, but winced when the movement caused pain. Rena noticed. "Go back to sleep. We will be here when you wake up."

I nodded and shut my eyes. I tried to go back to sleep, but after a few minutes I was about to give up. I was finally starting to drift off when I heard the door open. "How is she?" An unfamiliar male voice asked.

"She is still sleeping." Rena told the man.

"Good," he mumbled.

"Huh?" Rena asked. I heard thumping and the scrape of Rena's chair. I struggled to open my eyes again to see what was going on. After a few moments, I heard a whimper. My eyes flew open. Rena was being held against the wall by a really big man. He looked to be middle-eastern from his facial features and was wearing nurse scrubs. The man had one of his hands over Rena's mouth and with the other he was groping her. I sat up quickly, completely aware of the excruciating pain that ripped through my body. As he was going to undo his pants I ripped the IV out of my right hand and got to my feet. I wasn't going to let anything happen to my sister.

I hurried across the room as the guy turned around. He looked shocked to see me awake and out of bed. Using all of my force, I yanked him away from Rena. She fell to the ground and started to hyperventilate. I shoved him against the wall and punched him, then kneed him in the groin. All of a sudden, Rena let out a shrill scream. Momentarily distracted, he took the chance and hit me in the face. That just made it worse. I was completely pissed by then. I slammed him against the wall again. I could hear people running towards the room. I punched him again and again and then used my last little bit of strength to shove him into the window. The glass shattered. He was too big to fall through, but he was unconscious.

As quickly as it came, the adrenalin rush was gone and the pain was worse than ever. As I heard the door open, the darkness pulled me under again.

-X-

Beep. Beep. Beep. This was the second time I was woken up from that horrible beeping. But this time, I knew it was the machine monitoring my heart. This time it was easy to open my eyes. As they fluttered open, I heard the most wonderful voice in the world. "She's waking up," Zander said. I looked at him and gave him a small smile. "Hey baby. I'm glad to see that you're awake."

"Me too." I noticed that the IV had been moved to my left hand; the right, where it was previously connected, was bandaged. The oxygen lines running to my nose were still bothering me. "How's Rena?"

"She's fine. You saved her, Serenity. You have a gunshot wound and I'm sure you were in a lot of pain. But you built up the strength to help your sister," he said to me in wonder.

"Of course I did. I'm just awesome like that," I told him with a grin.

"Yes, you are," he replied and kissed my forehead. I glanced around the room. Shorty was sleeping on the small couch. I noticed that I had been moved to a new room because this window wasn't broken. I glanced toward the door and then did a double take.

Standing at the open door was my Dad holding three cups of coffee. He was staring at me with a small hopeful smile on his face. "Dad?"

"Oh, Serenity," he exclaimed. He sat the coffee down on a little table and rushed over to my bedside. "I'm so glad you are okay, honey," he said to me. "I'm so sorry about trying to make you marry those psychopaths. Please forgive me."

"It's okay, Dad, I forgive you. So...," I said, a little hesitant. "Have you gotten the chance to talk with Zander?"

My father let out a chuckle. "Are you trying to ask me if I know he's your husband?" I nodded. "Then yes, I know. And I've gotta say, you know how to pick the dorks," he joked. "But I approve of both of my son-in-laws. They are very lucky to have wonderful women like you and your sister."

I smiled at him. "So you aren't mad?"

"No, honey. I'm not mad."

Another voice entered the conversation. "She's awake?" I looked to the doorway to see Damien and Mike. Damien looked really happy to see me.

"You better give Damien some of your time, Ren," Mike told me. "He's been bawling his eyes out the entire time until just a little while ago." He giggled.

"Really?" I asked Damien. He nodded sheepishly. "Come over here and give me a hug, Damey. I missed my brother." He walked over to me, smiling, and gently put his arms around me, careful not to squeeze too hard. "I love you, Damey. But you shouldn't worry about me. Don't you know me enough to know that I wouldn't let those idiots win? I wouldn't give up. I have too much to live for." I smiled at him.

"Yeah, Ren, I know. But you just make it hard for people not to worry. You are more accident prone than anyone I know."

My father spoke up. "I'm sorry to break up the party, but can I have a few minutes to talk to my daughter alone?" They all said yes. Mike woke up Shorty and after they all gave me a quick hug, they left.

My father sat down in the chair that Zander had been sitting in and grabbed my hand. "I'm so proud of you, honey."

"Why would you be proud of me? I ran away and convinced Rena to come with me." He rolled his eyes at me.

"I'm proud of you because you did what you had to do for what you knew was right. And when your sister and your friends were in trouble, you risked your life to save them. And just a little while ago, even though you had just gotten out of surgery and were in extreme pain, again, you did what you had to do to save Rena. You are a great person, Serenity. I'm proud to have a daughter like you." I had never seen my father cry until now.

"Dad," I said hesitantly. I really didn't want to bring this up now, but I didn't want to forget.

"What, sweetheart?"

"I think you should talk to Rena. She thinks you avoid her because she looks like Mom. And you do. I've noticed. You don't know how bad it hurts her, Daddy. You are her father, and she feels neglected. We both do. You are like a ghost. I know you miss Mom, we all do. But we need you."

The look on his face was heartbreaking. I almost wished I could take back my words.

"I'm so sorry, Serenity. I didn't even realize. But I will do better, I promise. And I'll talk to Rena."

"Thank you, Dad. I love you so much." I squeezed his hand.

"I love you, too, baby. Your mother would have been so happy to have known the wonderful woman you have grown up to be." He smiled at me and gave me a hug.

Right then, I remembered why I wasn't paying attention enough to not get shot in the first place.

"Dad?" I asked.

"Yes, Ren?"

"Will you go ask Mike where my puppy is?"

CHAPTER TWENTY~THREE

Memories

"Zander, can you please bring me a burrito?" I absolutely loved Mexican food.

"You know you can't have solid food right now. I'm sorry, but you can't have a burrito."

"Please?" I whined. "I really, really, really want one."

"I'm sorry, Serenity, you can't have one. But I promise, as soon as you are allowed to have it, I'll bring you a huge, spicy burrito, okay?"

"Fine... can I at least have a cheese burger? I'm really hungry." Zander sighed and rolled his eyes.

"No solid foods, baby. And I regret to inform you that a cheese burger is in fact solid." He laughed. "Would you like me to bring you some soup?" I wrinkled my nose.

"How about some vanilla pudding? I want a lot of vanilla pudding." Okay, I was officially high on the morphine the doctor gave me.

"Okay, Serenity. I'll call Mike and tell him to pick up some vanilla pudding when he brings the puppy." Zander said with a chuckle.

"Yay!" I said with a giggle. Shorty chose that exact moment to come into the room.

"So, Ren, how do you like being high? Are you going to start smoking with me now?"

"No, fluffy, I'm not going to smoke with you."

"Fluffy?" He asked, raising one eyebrow.

"Yep," I giggled again. I was giggling a lot today. "You look like a giant poodle when you phase." I started laughing harder and soon Zander joined me.

"Well, there are a few draw backs to this amazing 'fro of mine, but I still love it."

"Yeah, we all know you love it," Zander said. Then Shorty's cell phone started to ring. He looked at the caller ID and looked back up at me, apologetically.

"It's Courtney. I should probably talk to her. She hasn't heard from any of us since prom."

"Go ahead, I'll be here when you get back." I told him.

"You better be," he told me with a smirk. "No more escape attempts." *I'm watching you*, he mouthed as he left the room. I giggled at the memory.

Flashback

"Ugh," I groaned. Being in the hospital was so boring. I needed something to occupy my time. No one else was in my room with me at the moment, so I had to fend for myself. I carefully sat up in bed, hissing at the pain that ripped through my stomach. I slid to the side of the bed and stood up slowly. I figured that if I didn't move my stomach so much when I walked, the pain wouldn't be so bad.

I walked over to the little table on the other side of the room where my personal belongings were. I grabbed my wallet and made my way out the door and down the hall without being noticed. I got into the elevator and went down to the main floor. I wandered around until I found a little book store. "Thank God," I breathed, as I walked inside. I looked around for a few minutes, until I found some interesting looking books.

I was surprised when I heard a voice shouting at me. "There you are, Serenity! Why aren't you in your room and in bed?" I turned to see Zane walking up behind me, and he looked pissed.

"I was bored, so I decided to come and find some books to read," I said in a small voice. His gaze softened.

"Serenity, you had everyone worried sick. Couldn't you have waited for someone to come back?" he asked.

"No... By then I would have died of boredom." He sighed and took the books away from me, walking to the front desk. "Zane, here's the money!" I called to him.

"No, Ren, I'll buy them." I started to argue but he walked away faster than I could keep up in my condition. When I finally caught up, he had already paid for them.

We left the store, and I started walking towards a little restaurant when he grabbed my arm. "What are you doing?" He asked.

"Getting some food," I answered. "I'm starving."

"No you are not. You are going straight back to your room and into that bed."

"No, I'm not. I'm getting food."

I started to walk towards the restaurant again. I was surprised when he turned and walked the other way. I didn't really care, so I went inside and got in line. A few moments later, Zane walked inside with a wheel chair and a roll of duct tape. He stopped right beside me. I narrowed my eyes.

"You wouldn't," I said to him. He gave me an evil grin.

"I would."

Before I had the chance to try and escape, he had me in the chair and was taping me to it. There was laughter throughout the restaurant. My face got warm, and I was sure it was blood red.

"Come on, Zane. Let me out!"

"Nope." He wheeled me out of the restaurant, to the elevators, and back to my room. I complained the entire way back. Almost every time we passed someone, I would hear a chuckle or a giggle. When we got into the room, everyone was there waiting. They took one look at my pissed expression and Zane's smirk and they all started laughing hysterically.

After everyone calmed down, they decided to get mad.

"Why didn't you just ask me to bring you some books?" Rena asked me.

"Because, Rena, you read erotic romance novels. I don't think I could stomach those right now." As Rena blushed, everyone was laughing again at her choice of reading materials.

End Flashback

The memory faded, "What's so funny?" Zander asked me.

"I was remembering my escape attempt."

He gave me a small smile. "You really scared the hell out of me, you know. I came in your room and you weren't here. The only thing I could think was, please, God, please tell me they didn't take her." His eyes were full of sadness. "I don't know what I would do without you." A single tear rolled down his cheek.

"I'm so sorry, baby," I told him, leaning in to kiss his tear away. "I didn't mean to worry you. I was just lonely and bored. I promise I won't do it again." I gave him a small smile. "So how about calling Mike and telling him about the pudding? And maybe I can try and guilt Dad into bringing me a burrito," I said to him with a laugh.

After again informing me about not being able to eat solid foods, he left to make his call. A few minutes later, Rena came into my room.

"Hey, Serenity. How are you feeling?"

"I'm okay, I guess. But I'm really hungry and no one will feed me," I said with a pout. Rena just laughed at me and sat down.

"I saw Zander in the hallway. He told me to tell you that he was going to pick up Mike and the puppy and that he would be back soon. He also said something about pudding." I let out a little giggle. "Since Dad is in our hotel room sleeping, I figured that I would take this opportunity to talk to you about something I probably should have a long time ago. Are you up for it?"

The sad, scared look on her face instantly sobered me up. "What is it, Rena? You can tell me anything." I grabbed her hand, comfortingly.

"It's about the day that mom died... You don't know the whole story," she said, as a tear ran down her cheek.

"Its okay, Sissy," I said. I only called her that when she was really upset. "Tell me."

"It was the beginning of the war between us and Nevada, and I was fighting a couple of male wolves. They were a lot older than me, and more experienced at fighting than I was, since I was only sixteen. They were playing with me, amusing themselves. They kept making it look like I could get away and then moving back in on me."

As Rena told the story, I was drawn in. I could see it perfectly in my mind, as if it were my memory instead of hers.

Flashback

She was backed into a corner, terrified. The two male wolves kept backing out a little, making it look like she could escape, but every time she tried, they moved forward again, blocking her. After a few minutes, they grew tired of playing around and stalked towards her. Rena was so scared that she couldn't hold herself in wolf form any longer. She phased into human form, and naked, she curled up with her back against the wall, hiding her face in her knees.

She jumped when she felt a hand on her shoulder. She looked up into the most menacing pair of black eyes that she had ever seen.

"Don't be frightened little one," he sneered, "this is only going to hurt... well, a lot actually." He let out an evil sounding chuckle while his friend put his hand over her mouth right as she was about to scream.

They shoved her hard against the ground and the first man violently raped her. She was screaming through the man's hand covering her mouth.

"Keep her quiet!" he whisper-yelled to his friend.

The pain was unbearable, though it only lasted a few minutes. After the first man was done, he traded positions with the other man. Only a few moments into her second rape, they all heard a loud, terrifying snarl and then a wolf grabbed the man who was on top of her and ripped him away. The wolf immediately ripped his throat out. The other man moved away from Rena and phased back into wolf form and began attacking her savior... Our mother.

All Rena could feel was the pain. She curled into a ball and sobbed, listening to the snarls and ripping sounds going on around her. She heard a horrible yelp, and then growls before the two wolves closest to her were silent. She opened one eye and peeked, looking through her fingers. She saw the male wolf dead about ten feet away from her and her mother standing beside it, having just turned human. She limped towards Rena, and dropped to her knees beside her.

"I'm so sorry, baby girl," she said, sobbing and pulling Rena to her. She didn't even pay attention to all of the blood flowing from her wounds. Right then, she just needed to hold her daughter. She rocked back and forth with Rena in her arms. "I'm so sorry, baby, Mommy's here now. I'm here," she kept murmuring to her.

She yelled our father's name. She saw him running to them, shoving through the fighting wolves all around them.

"Serena, what happened? What's wrong with Rena?" he asked.

"She was raped. Please get Serenity away from the fight and take

her to the house. Please, please, please. We have to get our babies away from here."

She stood up with a sobbing Rena in her arms, and ran out of the building and down the street to our house. Dad had found me, and we were running right behind them. As soon as we all made it into the house, Mom lay Rena down on the couch and covered her with the throw blanket. I came over and asked what was wrong with my sister.

"You don't have to worry about that, baby," my mother told me and pulled me into a hug. She knew that she wasn't going to make it much longer. Her wounds were too great and she had lost too much blood. She looked into my eyes and then into Rena's. "Girls, just remember I love you two more than anything." She kissed us both on the forehead and walked over to where my father was pacing.

"Honey," she whispered. She kissed him and murmured I love you, before collapsing in his arms. She died of blood loss before we could make it to the hospital.

End Flashback

Rena was still holding my hand when her story came to an end. Tears were flowing freely down both of our cheeks. "Now you know why I was frozen with fear when that man was attacking me earlier. And why I am usually terrified of men. And that I only smoke to forget."

"Oh, Rena. I'm so, so sorry," I whispered to her. I pulled myself up into a sitting position, ignoring the pain and hugged her tightly. We stayed in that position for a long time, just crying and holding each other.

CHAPTER TWENTY-FOUR

Going Home

Rena and I just sat there and cried for a while, not letting each other go. Soon, Rena had to go and meet Zane, so I was there alone, thinking about my mother's death.

Why hadn't my father told me? He was going to marry us into that same pack after something like that? I planned on giving him a piece of my mind after I was able to scream again. I didn't get to think about it for long.

Zander and Mike both walked in, Mike carrying my puppy and Zander carrying a 12-pack of vanilla pudding. I pushed away all of the depressing and horrible thoughts as Mike put my little husky in my lap.

"Hey baby girl, how are you?" I asked her in a baby voice. Zander laughed at me.

"What are you going to name her?" He asked as he scratched her head.

I didn't even have to think about it. "Serena."

We all sat around and talked, eating pudding. I kept sneaking little bites to Serena because I couldn't resist her puppy eyes. Soon, it was late and Mike and Zander had to go.

"I promise I will be back first thing tomorrow morning," Zander said. "I love you."

"Love you, too." I fell asleep quickly once I was alone.

One Week Later

Because I was a werewolf, I was healing pretty quickly and was being released. My Dad begged us to come back to California to live but we refused. We were going to stay in Virginia to finish high school, and then we were going to go to college. Tasha promised him that she would make sure we stayed out of trouble. He let us leave with the compromise that he would be popping in at anytime to check in on us. Before we left, he made sure to scare the crap out of Zane and Zander. No one would tell me, but I was pretty sure that he threatened their lives.

Tasha rented a car for her, Damien, Mike, and Shorty. Zane, Rena, and Serena rode with Zander and I. We made it back to Virginia after only a few days.

As soon as they walked through the door, my sister and her husband went to take naps, claiming that they were exhausted. I thought that they just didn't want to help clean up the mess in the living room and basement.

Rena

As soon as we walked into the house, I claimed to be tired and dragged my new husband upstairs. We entered his bedroom and I closed the door. I had a plan to get what I wanted and to get Zander and Serenity out of the house for a while.

Zane turned to question me. "What's with the escape? I know you aren't tired." I gave him an innocent look as I walked forward and placed my hands on his chest.

"Hmm. Well then, I have an idea." I shoved him backwards and he collapsed onto the bed. I straddled his lap.

"I think I like this idea," he mumbled.

I leaned down, whispering in his ear. "Honeymoon time."

~X~

Serenity

After I got the puppy settled in, I grabbed some cleaning supplies and headed down to the basement to start cleaning while Zander changed his clothes.

I was still in some pain, so it hurt to get down into the floor. I had managed to clean up most of the blood in the carpet when Zander came in.

"What are you doing?!" He exclaimed when he saw me on the floor.

"Uh... I'm cleaning blood out of the carpet. What does it look like I'm doing?"

"Serenity, you are going to pull out your stitches," he said as he helped me up. "I'll do this."

"I'm not going to make you clean up everything. It's not like Rena and Zane are going to help."

"*You* aren't making *me* do anything. *I* am making *you* sit down." He gently pushed me down onto the couch. "And you're right about Zane and Rena. From what I heard, I'm assuming that they are starting their honeymoon."

I scrunched my nose. "Okay, too much information. I really didn't want that image of my new brother and my sister in my mind." He laughed at me as I desperately tried to think about something else. Then a thought hit me and a huge grin spread across my face.

"Hey, Zander?"

"Hmm?"

"I just thought of another reason why I can't wait to have these stitches out." I waggled my eyebrows suggestively at him. He caught on and shook his head at me with a big smile on his face. Different fantasies of Zander and I were running through my mind until I heard a loud moan. I made a gagging face.

"Ew! C'mon Zander. This can wait. I need to get out of this house, like now. How about we go get that burrito now?"

We both rushed out of the house as quickly as we could to get away from our siblings.

-X-

After I was completely healed, we returned to school. We were asked a lot of questions about where we were and what we were doing. No one had the guts to ask, but I was sure they noticed our wedding rings.

When I had talked to Shorty a few days ago, he told me that Courtney had completely changed her look, but I didn't even imagine how much. When I walked into first period, I was completely shocked.

Courtney was sitting in her usual seat beside mine. Her hair had been dyed black and was cut in a crazy style. She was wearing a black tank top with a black and red skirt that had little pictures of voodoo dolls on it. Her outfit was completed with a black choker, red jelly bracelets, and red converse high tops with black skull print.

I walked to my seat and sat down. "Wow, Courtney. I like your new look. What brought it on?"

She smiled at me. "I don't know. I just decided to do it. I think it suits me." Her smile vanished. "I'm mad at you," was all she said before she pouted and faced forward.

I couldn't help it, I laughed at her childish reaction. I saw the corner of her lip turn up slightly in a hint of a smile. "Why are you mad at me?"

"Like you don't know," she sighed before she turned to me. "Why didn't you invite me to your wedding? I thought we were friends." That's what this was about?

"Courtney, we are friends. If it would have been planned, I would have invited you. It was a last minute thing. I didn't even know it was going to happen until we got to Nevada. I would never intentionally leave you out."

"Promise?" She asked.

"I promise." She reached over and hugged me.

I looked over at Zander, who had been watching the entire conversation with amusement. I poked him in the shoulder and turned towards the front of the classroom just in time for Mr. Kroh to walk in.

School passed by quickly and soon it was time to go home. Before we went back to the house, we decided to pay a visit to Greg Olden to let him know that we were okay.

It was a long drive to his house, but we found it with directions from Tasha. Greg Olden lived in a mansion almost as big as mine back in California. We were met at the front door by a butler, who escorted us to a sitting room where Greg was sitting with a little girl. I smiled at him when he looked up at us.

"Serenity! I'm glad to see that you were able to rescue your friends. Let me introduce you. This is my daughter Olivia. Olivia, this is Serenity, Rena, Zane, and Zander." He pointed to each of us. I walked up to her.

"Hello, Liv, nice to meet you." I shook her hand.

"Nice to meet you, too," she said before she skipped out of the room.

Greg spoke up, "I really am glad that you all got away unscathed."

"Not completely unscathed," I said with a small laugh. "I unfortunately got shot."

"Oh God. Are you okay?"

"Yes, I'm fine. We just wanted to visit and let you know that we got away, and that we reunited with my father. He was very understanding, and he even apologized."

"Well, that's just excellent!" He glanced at my left hand. "And I see you got married, too."

"Yes, we did. And we couldn't be happier," I said with a smile.

Greg insisted that we all stayed for dinner to celebrate. We met his wife, Muriel, and his son, Dimitri. Rena spent a lot of time talking to her and her husband. I could tell that they were getting along pretty well. I talked to Olivia most of the time. Dimitri seemed to be completely fascinated with Zander and Zane.

We were all having a good time mingling and eating a delicious meal when the butler came in and handed Greg an envelope. When he opened it and began to read, all of the blood rushed from his face.

"What is it, Greg?" Muriel asked, worried.

He looked up. He looked at Rena, Zane, Zander and I. "The werewolf council has told me to inform you that you all are being put on trial for the murder of Trevor and Matt Krate, along with several other wolves."

There was looks of shock all around the table. Well, it's a good thing we had lawyers in the family.

CHAPTER TWENTY-FIVE

The Trial

We were due in court a week after our dinner with Greg Olden. When I called my father and told him, he was furious, but me, I couldn't say I hadn't expected it. We murdered them, even if it was in self defense. My uncle, Samuel Landon, agreed to be our lawyer. Dad made some calls and had it arranged that the trial would in Virginia, instead of Nevada.

I had to call Damien, Tasha, Mike, and Shorty to let them know about the indictment, and to tell them the court date. They were surprised; they didn't think there was anyone left who could point a finger at us.

My father and uncle flew in and were staying at our house. Of course, Dad was breathing down our necks the whole time, not letting us be alone, even though we were married. He complained about any little mess in the house, but did admit that it was pretty nice. He even offered to buy it for us, but we declined, considering we would be going to college soon.

The day of court, we all met for breakfast, including Greg Olden and his wife. We all filled up over half the restaurant. After a lot of food and loud conversation, our food was paid for and we made our way to the court house.

When we walked into the court room, I was terrified about what would happen. After the trial started, they began to call witnesses. I was the first called. Once I was seated in the witness stand, I was sworn in.

"Do you, Serenity Noonan, swear to tell the truth, the whole truth, and nothing but the truth, so help you God?"

"I do." From where I was sitting, I could see everyone in the court room. Shorty, Mike, Damien, Tasha, Zane, Rena, and Zander were sitting with my uncle. My father, Greg Olden, and his wife were sitting in the rows of seating behind them.

My lawyer got up and walked over to me to begin questioning.

"Serenity, can you tell me why you, Tasha Kaynes, Damien Kaynes, Mike Laverey, and Torak Santiago went to Nevada on the night of the murder?" He asked.

"Yes, I can. Trevor and Matt Krate along with the others kidnapped my sister, Rena, her husband, Zane, and my husband, Zander. Trevor called me and told me where to go so we did."

"Why didn't you call the police?"

"Because he told me that if I did, he would kill them. And he was watching my house, so he would know if I did. So I just gathered up the group and we went."

"What happened when you got there?" He seemed genuinely curious about how we pulled it off.

"I went in alone and was led to the basement. Rena, Zane, and Zander were tied up, sitting on the floor. After exchanging a few words with Trevor, the only way to help them was through him. So I punched him in the face as hard as I could, and when he fell, I had to knock the gun out of some guy's hand who was about to shoot me. When I got the gun, I hit him in the side of the head with it and knocked him out. Another guy with a gun was about to shoot me, but Zander had pulled his feet around and kicked him in the back of the knees.

"By this time, Tasha, Damien, Mike, and Shorty were coming down the stairs. Trevor had gotten up and was coming towards me with the other gunmen in the room I pointed the gun at Trevor and told him not to move. I gave my gun to Mike and untied everyone's bindings. Then somehow, everyone was fighting... We won."

"After you got away, why didn't you go to the police then?"

"Because we knew we still weren't safe. We had to get married to be safe. If we were married, no one could hurt Zane and Zander considering we were the alpha's daughters. After that I was shot by another group of them, so we weren't really worried about going to the police."

After a couple more questions, he let me step down. He questioned Tasha, Shorty, Damien, and Mike. Their stories were pretty much like mine. When it was Rena's turn, I listened intently, because they never told us what happened before we got there.

"Rena, can you tell me what happened when you were kidnapped?"

"We were just sitting in the basement watching movies while Serenity went to get pizza. About ten minutes after she left, we heard the door opening. We figured it was her, so we just stayed where we were. When they opened the basement door, we knew it wasn't her smell, so we all jumped up. When they got downstairs, two men launched themselves at Zane. When Zander saw Trevor and Matt coming downstairs, he was furious.

"'Where's Serenity?!'" is what he yelled at them. Trevor tried to grab him, and Zander tried to hit him. Trevor punched him in the face and busted his lip. He kept struggling, even when Trevor pulled out a knife and cut his arm. They had to knock him out. Zane was already in the floor, unconscious. I was frozen in shock and fear. I couldn't fight them. I have a fear of men, so I couldn't move. They tied us all up and loaded us into the back of a van. Matt was driving, because Trevor stayed behind. I tried to beg them to let us go, but they wouldn't. I told them they were making a mistake, because Serenity would kick their asses when she found them." Rena was cut of by the judge banging his gavel against the table and I coughed to hide my chuckle.

"Watch your language, Mrs. Noonan."

"Sorry, Your Honor, I was just telling what I said."

He nodded. "Continue."

"They drove all the way to Nevada, only stopping for food and gas. All they gave us was water, they wanted us weak. They took us to the Krate house and put us in the basement. About a day after we got there, Trevor Krate arrived. He came into the basement to check on us, and then went back upstairs. Unless it was to take us to the restroom, no one came back until Trevor got a text message from Serenity on my cell phone. He came downstairs with the group that helped kidnap us to share the news. Trevor and Matt sat at a little table in the middle of the room while the call was made to my sister.

"They didn't talk long and I wasn't paying much attention to the conversation. I knew Serenity was probably telling him off. Trevor spoke a little louder into the phone and looked at me. "'Get here soon, Serenity, your friends are waiting,'" he nodded to the man standing next to me. He held a knife to my throat, making me scream. Then he quickly wrapped his hands around my neck, effectively choking off my voice. After making sure Serenity heard the scream, he hung up the phone. I knew he was making a mistake by taunting my sister.

"Trevor and Matt sat at the table playing cards while we waited for her. Not long after, my cell phone pinged, alerting a text message. Trevor read it and got a terrifying grin on his face. He sent one back and ordered one of the bigger men in the room to go open the gate and escort Serenity inside. A few minutes later my sister followed the man into the basement. As soon as she was down the stairs she had her arms around Zander whispering into his ear. She did the same for Zane and I, telling us that Shorty, Mike, Damien, and Tasha were here and that they were gonna get us out. After that, she stood up and faced Trevor.

"They made quick introductions. He made it clear that he wasn't going to let us leave, so she attacked. She was holding a gun at him when the others came running down the stairs. She passed the gun off to Mike and untied us. By the time we turned to everyone else, the fight had started. It was the only way we could all get out of there. After everyone in the basement was dead, we high tailed it out of there and went straight to Vegas," Rena finished.

"Thank you, Mrs. Noonan." Our uncle said. "You may step down."

Zander and Zane had their turn at the stand as well. There were no witnesses for the Krate brothers and the other wolves, so the other lawyer just presented the evidence. The judge called for a forty-five minute recess so the jury could deliberate. While on recess we got some lunch, making it back in time for the jury to return.

As we waited for court to go back into session, I was extremely nervous. I had started biting my nails, a habit I had gotten rid of years ago, waiting in agonizing suspense. This verdict was going to either ruin our lives, or let us live in peace. When the judge banged his gavel, asking for order in the court, Zander pulled me into a tight, reassuring hug.

Finally, the verdict came.

A member of the jury stood to read the verdict. "We find the defendants not guilty of first degree murder deeming their actions as self defense."

I had to cover my mouth to keep in my squeal of joy. We were found not guilty! We were finally safe. As soon as we were outside of the court house I let out a loud shriek and jumped into Zander's arms, letting him spin me around with a huge grin on his face. After he put me down we all shared a group hug in relief.

My uncle took us all out for dinner at his favorite restaurant to celebrate. We were all finally stress free and laughing and having fun for the first time in a long time. Dad told us that he had to leave tonight because there was some business he had to attend to. Since there were no Krates left, Rena, Zane, Zander, Shorty, Damien, Mike, Tasha, and I officially owned the Nevada territory. The others decided that they didn't want to run a territory, they handed full ownership to Zander and I. Dad was going to run it until we finished with college and were ready to take over.

After dropping my Dad off at the airport, Zander and I went home. We were worn out from all of the stress of the day.

Zander and I usually slept in his room, but we kept separate rooms just in case we fought or got annoyed with each other. That way, no one had to sleep on the couch.

It was weird, being married at seventeen, but it was fun, too. I liked to tease Zander by pointing out guys that I thought were cute. We still hung out with all of our friends, but we spent a lot more time together. We were truly in love with each other.

It was great seeing Rena and Zane together. He was the only guy she had ever opened up to. When I saw them looking at each other, I could practically see the love pouring out of their eyes.

I don't know if anything lasts forever, but for now, life was pretty damn good.

Epilogue

Four Years Later

Seven days before Christmas we were in our vacation home in Maine and still not ready. Zander was outside putting up the lights as I was in the kitchen with Zane, making hot chocolate. Rena still wasn't home and she went to pick up our take out an hour ago. The roads were pretty bad outside, so I was starting to get worried.

Soon, Rena's headlights flashed through the front windows and Zane and I both let out a sigh of relief. I heard her car door slam, and seconds later she threw open the front door. "Zander get in here!" She dropped the food on the table and squealed in excitement. "I have amazing news!"

"What is it?" I asked her as Serena bolted through the hallway to see what the commotion was. Seeing it was just Rena, she walked over, gave her hand a loving lick, and plopped down in front of the fireplace.

"Okay, this is big!" Rena said enthusiastically.

"What's big?" Zane asked, bemused.

"Me!"

I didn't get it. Then Rena rubbed her flat tummy affectionately and realization dawned on both Zane and I at the same time. He dropped backwards into a chair with a small smile. I couldn't rein in my excitement.

"Pregnant!" I yelled.

"What?" Zander shouted from the roof in a shocked voice. There was a thump, then I could her him rolling and lights ripping from the shingles. There was a small shout as he fell— but he didn't hit the ground. I ran out the door, knowing he probably thought that I was talking about me.

I walked out to see Zander hanging from the roof upside down by the lights wrapped around his ankle. "Hmm," I mused. "I thought that only happened in movies." He ignored my comment.

Who's pregnant?" He asked with a small glint of hope in his eyes that made me smile.

"Rena is," I told him as I started to climb the ladder.

"Congrads," he said as Zane stood under him, making sure he wouldn't hit his head. Up on the roof, I untangled the lights from his ankle and Zane caught his shoulders as he dropped. After I got back down, I told him that we would finish the lights together after our hot chocolate.

Three Years Later

Rena and Zane's son, Zev Noonan, was three years old and still hadn't phased. It was normal for a baby to phase for the first time during their second year of life, but sometimes they just didn't. They remained human. When Zev's third birthday went by with no sign of fur or a tail, we determined that he wouldn't change.

After seeing Zander's face when he though I was pregnant, I talked to him about it. We decided to try. It didn't happen right off the bat, it took a while. We lived in separate houses now, Zander and I alone. Rena and Zane came over frequently for visits, always bringing little Zev. I had been sleeping much more than usual, and

I had been eating a lot. One day after work I stopped at the drug store to buy a few pregnancy tests. When I got home, I stuffed my bag into my jacket and ran inside, heading straight to the bathroom. As I passed, I saw Rena and Zane on my couch, Zev playing with Serena. Zander was probably in the kitchen.

Once I closed the door, I locked it and pulled out my bag. I had bought three tests for accuracy. After using them, I sat them on the sink to wait. After two minutes, Rena started banging on the door.

"Serenity! Hurry up, I have to pee!"

"Hang on a minute!" I yelled back.

It seemed like forever until I could check the tests. I had bitten my fingernails down to the quick in anticipation. "Hurry up, Ren! What's taking you so long?" Rena was still outside the bathroom door.

I picked up the first test and was confused at the results. I picked up the others and checked them too. Why hadn't I just picked a simple one that just said pregnant or not pregnant? Of course I hadn't wasted time by reading the instructions.

"What the hell do two blue lines mean?" I yelled. Rena's squeal was all the answer I needed.

Four Years Later

We had named our daughter Claire after Zander and Zane's mother. She was beautiful. She had jet black hair and Zander's hazel eyes. Zander was the happiest man in the world when she was born. He still is. He never complained and whenever he talked about her, which was always, his eyes lit up.

Claire was the sweetest thing ever, so she definitely took after her father, because I could be a bit of a hot head. She loved to follow Zev around, and pull on his bright red hair. For a seven year old, he put up with his little cousin well.

We were all more than surprised when I got a call from Courtney, telling me that we were all going to meet because she had some news. Shorty, Courtney, Damien, Mike, Zander, Claire, and I were all meeting at Rena and Zane's house for lunch. I was also surprised to get a call from Rena right as we were about to leave.

"Hello?" I asked into the phone as I struggled to get the jacket on Claire's squirming form.

"Serenity!" She said frantically. "Zev blew up!"

Rena

"Mommy, can you make me some chicken noodle soup?" Zev asked me.

"Sure, Sweetie," I answered. He had had a cold for a few days now. After he ate, I was going to put him to bed so he wouldn't be bothered by the people coming over. After putting the soup on, I turned back to Zev. As he let out a sneeze, he exploded into a mound of red fur. After a moment, I realized I was looking at a puppy. He was alarmed. He started running around and crying.

"Oh my God, my baby!" I was in shock. After failing at calming him down, I did the only thing I could think of. Zane wasn't home from work yet, so I called my sister.

"Hello?" She asked.

"Serenity! Zev blew up!"

"What?"

"He just sneezed and turned into a wolf. I can't get him to calm down,"

"I'll be there in a minute." She hung up.

I chased him around the house for a few minutes and finally caught him in the living room. I tried to hold him but he wouldn't stop squirming. Serenity walked into the house and saw me trying to hold him to my chest. She came over and snatched him out of my arms.

"Rena, you red head! You have no soul," she said to me in mock anger as she scratched behind his ears. He calmed down instantly.

"Hey," I replied. "He has red hair, too."

"Well, he takes after his father," she retorted as she set him down. I noticed that Claire was phased too. She trotted over to him and nudged him with her nose. "See? It's fine. He was just late."

"Yeah, yeah," I said as they ran out the dog door installed for Serena.

"Why are Zev's clothes shredded in the floor?" Zane asked as he walked in the open front door.

"He phased," Serenity answered. He looked at me in shock.

"Really?"

"Yep," I told him.

Zander hadn't even bothered to speak. He had just plopped down on the couch and turned on a football game.

"Well now that the excitement is over, I need to start lunch," I said.

"Rena, please just order some food. I'm too tired to rescue your kitchen again," Serenity begged.

"Fine," I surrendered as there was a knock on the door. Zane let Shorty, Courtney, Damien, and Mike inside. I called and ordered some food before joining everyone in the living room.

"So, I have some news," Courtney said as I sat down. "Shorty and I are getting married!" Serenity choked on her soda.

"Really?" She shouted. "That's awesome!" The excitement was cut short as Zev and Claire darted into the room. Everyone had worried looks as Zev phased behind the couch to hide his body.

"Mom! Isn't it awesome? I can phase!" All of out heads whipped to where Courtney was sitting. She had a smile on her face.

"Geez, I feel like I'm going to be 'silenced'. Don't worry, I already knew. Frankly, I'm hurt no one told me. Especially you." She gave Shorty a look. He looked sheepish.

"Well how did you know?" Zander asked her.

"I'm not human either. I'm a—."

Sydney Pennington is a teenage girl with a passion for reading and writing fiction. She is currently a high school student and lives in South Point, Ohio with her mother, little sister, and dog. This is her first book.